"Mark Sundeen dips his pen in the blood of the bull to make literature full of life and lust. Also, he makes his mom sound nice."

—Sarah Vowell, author of *The Partly Cloudy Patriot*

"Well-turned ambiguities, delivered with the steady patter of a late-night TV host's extended comic monologue."

—*Kirkus Reviews*

"[An] amusing, chivalric tongue-in-cheek story . . . *[The Making of Toro]* is a skewed travelogue, in which the line between a gritty reality and a chimerical fantasy is warmly blurred."

—*Publishers Weekly*

Praise for *Car Camping*

"A riotous, beautiful, totally original road novel masquerading as a travel book. Sundeen's America . . . shimmers with life. The prose is pure, wild, naive, and poetic—a brilliant and auspicious debut."

—George Saunders

"A wonder of a book, Mark Sundeen is a stunningly wonderful writer. This book is to be savored and remembered."

—Hubert Selby, Jr.

PASSION . . . "Then take this," she moans. She presses the bull's ear into his palm. "Today it is warm and filled with blood, like my heart. When it turns hard and dry, Travisito, remember the heart of little Carmen."

DANGER . . . "Viva la causa!" says Comandante Felipe. "We march together as friends."

"No, hermano," says Travis LaFrance. "We march as brothers."

ADVENTURE . . . "How does a dame like yourself make a buck?" says LaFrance.

"Adult films."

Right answer, he thinks. "Let's get a drink."

LITERATURE . . . The owl beckons him thither, southward to the border. There's no turning back. Ask not for whom the owl hoots, Travis.

Such are the morsels that feed the soul of Travis LaFrance, hero of the acclaimed bullfighting classic *Toro: Encounters With Men and Bulls: An Aficionado's Odyssey from Tijuana to Mexico City and Back.*

TRAVIS LaFRANCE

FALCONER . . . LOVER . . . AFICIONADO . . . AUTHOR

His romances are legendary
His journeys are unforgettable
His escapades are thrilling
His prose style is brilliant

HIS ART IS HIS LIFE, AND VERSA VICE

THE MAKING OF TORO
A Simon & Schuster Book

THE MAKING
OF TORO

ALSO BY MARK SUNDEEN

Car Camping: The Book of Desert Adventures
Salt Desert Tales (with Erik Bluhm)

ALSO BY TRAVIS LaFRANCE

Fun with Falconry
*Toro: Encounters with Men and Bulls: An Aficionado's Odyssey
from Tijuana to Mexico City and Back*
Cocksman in Silhouette: An Autobiography (forthcoming)

THE MAKING OF TORO

BULLFIGHTS, BROKEN HEARTS, AND ONE
AUTHOR'S QUEST FOR THE ACCLAIM
HE DESERVES

MARK SUNDEEN

SIMON & SCHUSTER
NEW YORK · LONDON · TORONTO · SYDNEY

FOR MOM AND DAD

 SIMON & SCHUSTER
Rockefeller Center
1230 Avenue of the Americas
New York, NY 10020

First Simon & Schuster trade paperback edition 2004

SIMON & SCHUSTER and colophon are registered trademarks
of Simon & Schuster, Inc.

For information about special discounts for bulk purchases,
please contact Simon & Schuster Special Sales:
1-800-456-6798 or business@simonandschuster.com

Photographs by Anna Hrnjak
Manufactured in the United States of America

1   3   5   7   9   10   8   6   4   2

The Library of Congress has cataloged the hardcover edition as follows:

Sundeen, Mark, 1970–
The making of toro : bullfights, broken hearts, and one author's
quest for the acclaim he deserves / Mark Sundeen.
p.   cm.
1. Americans—Mexico. 2. Bullfighters.
3. Bullfights. 4. Authorship.
5. Mexico. I. Title.

PS3619.U55 M3 2003
813'.6—dc21   2002030403

ISBN: 978-0-7432-5563-9

I know who I am, and who I may be, if I choose.
—DON QUIXOTE DE LA MANCHA

CHAPTER ONE

———

THE NEWS THAT I WAS TO WRITE A BOOK about bullfighting came after a morning spent emptying tubs of human poo. You might think that in this age of talking toasters and the programmable toothbrush, science would provide a machine for this chore, but no: My only tools were gravity, scrub brush, and a garden hose. The plastic tubs were white and heavy like little ovens, cooking with the waste of twenty-five people who had just rafted for a week down the Colorado River. Beneath the seat was an opening big enough to insert your head, and on the ground where the poo had to go was a hole no wider than my fist.

Before becoming the author of an excellent but over-looked adventure book, I had considered this work filthy and dehumanizing—beneath me, actually—and I would have demanded that the guides clean it themselves. But events in the last year had changed my opinion. Under the name of Travis LaFrance I'd published a slim paperback about hunting for desert rodents with highly trained falcons, a brilliant little book really, not at all about birds if you could read between the lines but rather a deft song of the self in the guise of a swashbuckling how-to. *Fun with Falconry* is triumphant, soaked in the sauce of boyish lyricism but fried tough in a cynic's skillet. I recommend it.

But so convincing was my book of meta-falconry that the literati could not crack its facade. "Unfortunately there is no plot," wrote one newsman, a dim observation he'll regret until some merciful downsizing at headquarters ends his ill-chosen career. Meanwhile, the book flew over the heads of the bird-of-prey trade magazines, and despite my dreams of seeing Travis LaFrance leaning against Jack London on the Literature shelf, *Fun with Falconry* was exiled by booksellers to the Animal Husbandry alcove, doomed to obscurity along-side *Tricks for Turtles* and *An Introduction to Llama Packing*.

So instead of spending the summer rubbing my chin on book shows and rubbing the knees of ripe coeds who would endure around-the-block waits for an autograph— instead of that, I had returned to my honorable job in the hot Utah desert and was currently faced with the prospect of moving poo from a plastic tub to a hole in the ground. I'd taken this job with the promise that I'd be rowing boats by the end of the season, but three years later I'd proven so indispensable around the yard that the boss couldn't afford to lend me to the river.

Luckily literature had paid me in a spiritual currency more rare than job advancement. "My art is my life, and versa vice," says *Falconry*'s stoic hero, and adopting Travis LaFrance's creed as my own, I had discovered the virtuosity of poo disposal. Since the book's publication I had even be-gun volunteering to do it, a development that had not only fortified my character but delighted my co-workers, who were too simple to understand me.

There is a relatively sanitary method to the task. By fas-tening a tube you can drain the box into the sewage hold

without ever seeing its contents. But I had forsworn this tube
as a cowardly apparatus. I wanted to be more like Travis
LaFrance, who instead of wincing at destiny grabs it bare-
handed and molds it into something beautiful.

My method was pure, expressive, a triumph of both
form and function. I set the box on the concrete pad, kicked
it once to its side, kicked it twice upside down, then lifted.
The box had been topped off with water earlier in the day
to loosen the clumps, and now with a great sucking sound
there erupted a terrific mountain of shit and toilet paper
and tampons and maggots, spilling green rivulets of septic
chemical down its ravines. Some of my co-workers, like
rubes in a fine art gallery, simply can't fathom the beauty:
They gasp, they gag, they cover their eyes. But I looked on
calmly. With my discriminating eye I saw a robust palette
of raw tempera awaiting the infusion of human spirit.

"Jimbo," I called, as he happened to walk by. "Have you
seen The Scepter?"

"You mean that nasty broom handle?"

"I mean The Scepter."

"In the Dumpster, where it belongs."

It was 100 degrees and I was sweating in my rubber
boots and plastic apron and elbow-length dishwasher gloves.
Though sometimes the poo is sufficiently soft to be gulped
up by the hole in a single prolonged swallow, today as
usual we had a clog. I had left The Scepter here in my studio for these occasions, but some unenlightened simp had
apparently tossed it. Sifting through the garbage I retrieved
the slender oaken staff, gripped it tightly so that our spirits
might mingle, and then like Jackson Pollack stirring his
bucket I plunged it forcefully through the shit heap. It was
just the thing. The heap coughed, I aimed the hose, and then

with a spit and a sublime gurgle the poo was slurped into the earth.

A good morning's work. I rinsed the boxes, slapping to dislodge the lonely corn kernel, then bleached the units and set them to dry. I peeled off my protective layers and washed. Saying good-bye to the guides still busy with such pedestrian tasks as washing pots and scrubbing coolers, I pitied for a moment their artless lives, then drove home to my trailer. Catching a whiff of sewage, I sniffed myself and checked my shoe soles, but didn't find any residue.

Before I reached the shower I discovered the message from New York concerning a book. Don't think I'm some hack who lets the latest glossy gazette charter me a camel ride or spelunking tour. I am an artist. Whereas young men in other generations have measured their courage by enemy gunfire, my imagined crucible concerned that inevitable million-dollar offer: Would I stand true to my craft and refuse it or would I sign on the line and go to hell with the rest of the sellouts? So before making the phone call I scrubbed to the elbows for the third time and resolved to accept no work that would demean me.

The agent and I had never met. He was a voice on the line who reported now and then that, like the work of any misunderstood visionary, my writing had not sold. My records showed that he'd earned $64.57 from our arrangement the previous year, and I imagined him at lunch in a fancy bar and grill boasting to all the other agents about the satisfaction of representing a true master. "I used to value money like you do," he'd scold them, "but that was before I found a higher calling." The other agents would sulk back to their plush offices feeling at once the hollowness of their riches and a new inspiration to exalt literature to the people.

And now things were turning around, said the agent when his assistant finally took me off hold and patched me through. A publisher wanted to pay me to write a book.

"A book about what?"

"Bullfighting."

I had never been to a bullfight.

"Are we talking six figures?" I said.

"Not quite."

"High fives?"

"Nope."

"Medium fives?"

"Upper fours," said the agent.

I did not figure that minus the agent's cut my total payment for *Toro* would be about seven thousand dollars. My mind computes moods, not numbers. I did not consider how much it would cost to get to the part of the world that has bullfights and live there long enough to write a book, and I certainly did not calculate how quickly I could earn that same sum in the boatyard. In a flicker of fantasy I saw the name Travis LaFrance emblazoned on another book jacket, topping the critics' top-ten lists, headlining the program for the White House reception. The more I considered a winter in Moab collecting unemployment and applying for heat assistance, the more I realized that, yes, what literature really needs at this moment is a book about bullfighting by a young white American man, and that accepting such a small advance would not be the soulless money grab of a sellout, but on the contrary would constitute proof that my work transcended monetary value. Without a hesitation I said:

"I'll do it."

*   *   *

The result, once I iron out a few wrinkles with the publisher, will be *Toro: Encounters with Men and Bulls: An Aficionado's Odyssey from Tijuana to Mexico City and Back.* Its phenomenal success will astound everyone but me. By the time you read this, *Toro* will have already had a long surf atop the bestseller charts, Travis LaFrance will be a talk-show staple, and critics will have talked themselves hoarse pronouncing him the next Ernest Hemingway.

Since you're reading *The Making of Toro,* you've surely read *Toro* and want to learn about the man behind Travis. If not, you'll pop down to your bookseller, where stacks of LaFrance are disappearing by the crateload, but for now a bit of background will help. Here's the proposal I wrote after the phone call from the agent, which with a few minor edits will grace the bestselling dust jacket.

> Ernest Hemingway. Pablo Picasso.
> Great artists and great men, united by a passion for fine women, high adventure, and la fiesta brava. In *Toro: Encounters with Men and Bulls: An Aficionado's Odyssey from Tijuana to Madrid,* falconer Travis LaFrance takes us on a voyage through the 21st-century remnants of the Spanish empire, in search of the flickering flame of manhood imported from Iberia five centuries ago.
> His quest begins in Tijuana, the northernmost outpost of the Kingdom of Carlos, where the blood of the bulls mingles with the sweat of the laborer on his journey toward el norte. Making his way by train, burro, and thumb through the dusty villages, lured by cold cerveza and strong tequila and lusty señoritas, the ever-hardy LaFrance blends the drama and artistry of the bullring with his rich tales of love and loss, and reveals that, yes, beyond that familiar realm

of the starched-shirt pencil-pushers, in a land more
primitive and passionate than his own, there does
yet exist a small yet robust sample of that endan-
gered species known as man.

Toro pierces the heart of la fiesta brava, the soul
of Mexico and Spain, and not least of all the spirit of
Travis LaFrance.

A month has passed since I shipped the finished manuscript of Toro, and the publisher's silence has been like that
of a stunned bullring after a flawless kill. But I won't post-
pone my victory lap waiting for those New York judges to
wave a green handkerchief. No matter how great the book
is, no one will read it if they don't hear about it, and I
vowed early that Toro would not slip into the same cracks
that held Fun with Falconry. Having seen television shows
like "The Making of Titanic," I know that a blockbuster is
not the work of some recluse behind a typewriter, but the
result of slick marketing that hypes the final product as so
fabulous that it merits a documentary on its very creation.
What works for movies should work for books, and so as I
set out to write Toro I also began this behind-the-scenes
memoir of the forging of a classic. Call it a companion
piece to genius.

So join me, reader, and learn how an average soul like
myself has invented a legend. Do not be dismayed to learn
that, like you, I am imperfect and fallible. Do not be disappointed that I am not the man whom you have come to ad-
mire and envy. Rather, as we study the evolution of our
hero, take heart that even I, his creator, strive each day to
be a bit more like Travis LaFrance.

CHAPTER TWO

———

TO WRITE A BOOK ABOUT BULLFIGHTING I
needed to learn something about bullfights. As winter fell
in Utah I ordered some expensive books and began reading. Within a month I was, in all modesty, an expert.

I began to write, first summarizing the conclusions *Toro*
would eventually reach:

Concerning el Mundo Latino, Travis LaFrance would
discover that Mexico is a land rich in romance and history,
where if you close your eyes at night you can hear the foot-
steps of the Maya padding barefoot across the desert. Same
goes for Spain. Like Travis, the Latinos are a people gov-
erned by primeval passion, spirit, and tradition, uncorrupted
by the materialism of the norteamericanos. Travis would
choose a burro and a serape any day over a stucco duplex
with two and a half bathrooms.

And concerning bullfighting, Travis would discover an
ancient ritual almost indecipherable to Americans. Half
artist and half athlete, the bullfighter combines bravery
with finesse, strength with dance. We Americans who come
from such a superficial culture might consider the fiesta
brava gruesome or barbaric, but who are we to criticize?
Maybe if Americans had a healthy outlet for our repressed

blood lust and a more natural acceptance of cycles of life and death, Travis will wryly note, maybe then we wouldn't be always shooting each other with machine guns at the post office.

And concerning the great metaphor between writing and bullfighting, Travis after much reflection will come to understand that both artists labor for years at a craft that is rarely understood by the masses. They confront pain not only with courage, but with flourish. And just as a writer's masterpiece may be trashed by small-minded critics, a matador may give his very soul to a bull and still be panned in the next morning's papers by jealous newsmen too cowardly to enter the ring. While thousands may attempt with the pen and with the sword, only a handful will actually succeed in either of these great pursuits.

Having already reached such canny conclusions, there was little reason to even go to Mexico or Spain. I could have continued the research and written the book from home, and frankly that would have suited me fine. I don't really like traveling. Unlike Travis LaFrance, bighearted ambassador of unity and togetherness, I could not care less about other cultures, especially not in the third world. Sure: I am impressed when someone comes home from Zimbabwe and brags that he was the only American or, better yet, the only white person in the whole place, but sometimes I wonder why all the effort. If you want to be the only white person, you don't even need to leave Los Angeles. Just get on a bus. So while others roam the globe looking to be accepted into someone else's tribe, to smoke their peace pipe or do their Quetzal dance or eat of the sacred bascayabaya melon, the only tribe I ever wanted to join was my own, and I haven't even been able to figure out if I have one.

I blame my parents for this disability. By age nine I'd already had my fill of the third world. Dad was a college professor who every six years took a sabbatical to teach in some far-off foreign place. When I was three it was Sweden, and I can't really count this as exotic, because everyone looked like me and besides I have only a few memories: picking strawberries in a sunny field and eating fresh shrimp just off a boat in a harbor. One night we ran over a drunk who stepped in front of the rented Saab, but to this day my parents insist that the man was hardly injured in what was for me a modestly traumatic moment.

Then in 1979 my parents began planning their next adventure and decided we would spend six months somewhere called Iran, and we certainly would have, if not for the trend of hostage-taking that suddenly developed. The plan was scrapped, and with just a few months remaining before his sabbatical, my father scrambled for a new assignment. As a result, in the early part of 1980 my family deplaned in Port Moresby, the capital city of Papua New Guinea, a country that weeks earlier none of us could have located on a globe (it turns out to be an island just north of Australia, if you're wondering).

Shortly before our departure, Mom had come home from the camping store with four matching duffel bags, one per person—red, yellow, green, and orange—and instructed my brother and me to pick a color and fill it with whatever we thought we might need for six months in the jungle. So at the airport when someone from the university finally arrived in a microvan to greet us, we were waiting somewhat dazed on the tarmac clutching our plump luggage like

blond-headed, blue-ribbon farmers at the county fair—
a pumpkin for me, a watermelon for Dad, a squash for
Mom, and a grand-prize tomato for Richard. My brother
and I wore incredibly loud Hawaiian shirts freshly purchased during our three-day layover in Honolulu, a vaca-
tion that years later I would recognize as the old bait and
switch: "Hey, kids! We're going to Hawaii! For three whole
days!" And for an added bonus, you'll spend the next six
months living in a house on stilts in a country you've never
heard of.

The degree to which my parents had no idea what they
were doing was not evident until twenty or so years later,
when my dad and I were recalling that day at the airport
and he suddenly rubbed his brow and said something totally unexpected: "It wasn't until then that it hit me—I
guess I'd known it, but I hadn't really understood it fully—
that the people there were going to be black."

So there we were, white, in the house on stilts across
the street from the university, my brother and I attending
the international school mixed with Australians, Filipinos,
British, and a few Papua New Guinea nationals. We were
the only Americans, a mark accentuated by our parents' re-
fusal to buy the required green-and-gray school uniforms.
Their decision was purely economical, but firmly supported
by my brother and I, who thought uniforms were for dorks.
My parents subscribed to a child-rearing philosophy man-
dating that as soon as a boy could dress himself he could
choose his own wardrobe, so Richard and I arrived on the
first day of classes with feathered haircuts, adorned in the
traditional garments of the California beach suburbs: two-
tone corduroy shorts, white tube socks with stripes, custom

Vans skateboard shoes, and wide-collared surfscape shirts with wooden buttons and lightning bolts on the sleeves. I don't recall any of our fellow students recognizing the degree of fashion we modeled; My brother, who was twelve and capable with his fists, had to throw a couple of punches to defend our culture.

My parents' scorn for school uniforms was just the beginning of what I now identify as their seriously flawed raising of a child destined to be the adventure traveler Travis LaFrance. How was I to rebel later in life against a straitlaced upbringing when at age nine I was already allowed to wear whatever tasteless clothing I could choose? And how could I long for a taste of the exotic when before fifth grade I'd already been dragged out to Loloato Island, where we snorkeled on top of the Great Barrier Reef and my brother and I learned that a sharp kick to a sea cucumber caused it to ooze spaghetti-like things from one end? I remember going inside a live volcano, climbing atop downed World War II bombers, sinking deep into an underground labyrinth of Japanese army bunkers, guided by the British son of one of Dad's colleagues. The lad thought it would be funny to scare Richard and me by turning off the flashlight and leaving us there, only to be disabused of this notion when my valiant brother collared him in the darkness and bloodied his nose, leading to considerable embarrassment and apologies by my parents and to secret pride and making of the Hang Loose hand sign by my brother and me. On another of Dad's so-called research excursions, one of his students took us to his village in the highlands—he was the first from his tribe to attend college—and the villagers hurried out to run their fingers through the hair of the only blond children they had ever seen. Later our host led us to a cave, the village burial chamber, and held a candle over the mummies, the most recent of which was his own mother, still wrapped in blankets.

And then came the trip home. No, we couldn't just fly back to Hawaii and lie on the beach and watch the girls dance. Onward to Bali, Singapore, Malaysia, Thailand, Hong Kong: a spree of beds without sheets and baths without water, toothless masseuses in palm-frond huts and excitable drivers of three-wheeled taxis, unrecognizable carcasses hanging in restaurants followed by unidentified meat pieces on a plate with rice. By age ten I'd collected a life's worth of third-world travel, and before I finished high school my parents took me back to Indonesia and all across Mexico, up the pyramids at Chichen Itza, through the subways of Mexico City.

And there were the potlucks at home. Both my parents taught foreign students, and at end-of-term parties I sampled kimchi and satay and curries and briyanis, and met people with dots on their faces and turbans on their heads, not even aware that I was being broadened, experiencing multiculturalism in my own home, but instead squirming for the OK from Mom and Dad to excuse myself from the smorgasbord and shuttle the little black-and-white TV to the back bedroom and watch the *Dukes of Hazzard* like any regular American.

Later in life my mother continued to flaunt her worldliness by traveling to Guatemala, first on one of Dad's sabbaticals, then starting a business of importing woven things, returning three times a year, bumping along mountain roads in chicken buses, bartering in broken Spanish with a

Dixie accent—what she lacks in language skills she compensates for in excellent facial expressions and hand gestures. So when someone tells me about hiking to Peruvian mountain villages and learning to weave, I think: Big deal, my mom does that.

In short, by being so goddamned open-minded my parents deprived me of my right, as a disaffected collegiate, to reject American materialism and go searching for myself in the third world. As an adult I would gain no thrill from bargaining for trinkets in pidgin English. Never could I grow a beard and trek through Nepal reading Hermann Hesse, sink into a teahouse and scribble in my journal:

> I'm beginning to realize that despite what I've seen on television, most people in the world are not white. In fact, we're the minority on this planet. I'm learning that other cultures are very colorful, and different, in a good way. But deep down, I think we are all of the same race: the human race.

All the more reason why I had to invent bighearted Travis LaFrance to report back from the jungles and ranchos of Mexico, befriending natives and spreading goodwill. He's not so cynical as I am, and would never look back at his travels and wonder who gives a shit about what some middle-class American has to say about the world, and Travis would never despair that it's all been said, done, and written about before.

So I planned for Travis the quest of a true believer: from north to south, from the rational to the primitive, from the distant echoes of the fiesta brava to its pounding heart. By the time winter ended, I was three months behind in my rent, but I had all the details in place, and I finally called the publisher to find when the check would arrive so I could set out.

"Are you in Mexico City yet?" asked the publisher. "We haven't heard from you in months."

"I'm in Utah."

"You're already back?"

"I've already written a few chapters. What happened to that check?"

"You mean you haven't left yet?" said the publisher. "You signed the contract four months ago."

"I'll be in Tijuana next week."

"But the Tijuana season is already over. It ended in November. At this rate you'll miss Mexico City, too."

I couldn't reason with a man who suffered from such lack of imagination. When the check finally came I paid my back rent and credit card bills, leaving some two thousand dollars to write the book. For economy's sake, I scrapped the original proposal—the quest, the narrative progression, the back roads, and the out-of-the-way places—and with a single phone call bought a one-way plane ticket from Los Angeles to Mexico City. I'd worry later about getting to Spain.

And so I began my journey, not with the moonlight donkey ride across the border that you remember from *Toro*, but with an overnight drive to my parents' house in California. After snowstorms on the Navajo Nation, I found myself settling down to sleep in the back of my truck in a muddy field behind an Arizona truck stop. As the jake brakes rumbled on the interstate and the headlights flashed through my camper shell, I lay in my sleeping bag and wrote that memorable opening to Chapter One:

The desert night is as still and quiet as a freshly killed carcass. Not a light, not a sound, not even a noise. Somewhere south of here, across la frontera, a Mexican owl hoots.

"Vamanos," I say to Rocinante, draping the blanket across her bony back. "Time to go."

The burro's ears perk up as the owl hoots again.

"I don't know, Roxie. Who do *you* think he's talking to?"

We ride along in the darkness. We don't know where we're going, but we damn sure know where we've been. There's no turning back now. The owl beckons us thither, southward.

Ask not for whom the owl hoots, Travis. It hoots for thee.

CHAPTER THREE

UNLIKE THE SHALLOW PEOPLE OF MY GEN-
eration obsessed with fame, Travis LaFrance doesn't care
a lick about how he's remembered. He lives only in the
moment. Of course, Travis has the advantage of being a
character in several soon-to-be classic books, and since his
words and deeds are guaranteed to live eternally, he doesn't
need to fret.

For the rest of us, living forever is a lot of work, and
there is nothing shallow about it. What could be more profound than being remembered by the whole world? The
purpose of my time on Earth is to get material for books,
the purpose of writing books is to get famous, and the purpose of fame is to live forever.

The shallow ones are those who mistake fame for eternal life. Fame is like purgatory, a waiting period while it's
determined whether you'll go on to immortality. While
you're there you get benefits, like praise and money and
worldly women. If along my way to heaven I'm to be loved
by a million readers of a million books, so be it. No reason
to turn down the perks.

Driving toward Los Angeles, the city that makes celebri-
ties, I indulged a small daydream of how the news of my

second book contract would shake the town. In elite circles I was already well known as the native son who had co-founded *Western Dude* magazine, then hit the big time with *Falconry*. *Dude*'s co-editor lived in L.A. and was intimately connected with the art scene. Henry even worked at a gallery, his creative tasks ranging from hanging masterpieces to painting walls to mopping up spilled champagne at the openings. I imagined myself at such a reception, surrounded by slim-hipped women in high-heeled sandals who wanted to know who my influences were, and I'd tell them it all began with Turgenev, and that literature of the soil was born in Russia. We'd call for another bottle and they'd say what about Tolstoy, so we'd talk about him and maybe I'd switch it over to Norway and say a few words about good old Knut Hamsun, too.

And that very night I found myself at Henry's gallery and the women were just as I'd envisioned. They invited Henry to join them at the festival at Echo Park, but he had to stay and clean up.

"But I can come," I said, just in the nick of time.

"My car's full," said the girl. "You can meet us there if you want."

The evening was quickly turning fabulous. The lotus flowers in Echo Park bloomed big enough to swallow a man whole, and the fireworks burst overhead like my signature scrawled in the sky. The girls sat cross-legged in the grass beside the glassy pond with a Ferris wheel spinning overhead. They wore crisp jeans and spaghetti straps and heart-shaped sunglasses propped on their foreheads. They had exciting names like Esmerelda and Stella and Ophelia, and when I asked what they did, they said photography or film or visual arts, and I knew right away they'd appreciate a craftsman like myself.

Let's go on the Ferris wheel, said someone, and I strolled into the crowd along the lake with Stella. Toy guns went *pop* at the shooting range and somebody won a stuffed animal. Stella said later we'd go to a party in the hills that was invite-only but Emil and Elena would call on the cell and give directions and sneak us in.

"I'd like to see your work sometime, Stella."

"It can't be seen."

"It's not finished?"

"It's not meant to be viewed."

"What do you do with it?"

"It's like: contextual."

"Oh."

"I'm getting an MFA. Shit, we lost the others."

"We'll find them soon enough," I said, imagining with a thrill that we were stranded together for the evening.

"I'll just call." She pulled her phone from her handbag and pressed a button. "Ophelia, where are you?"

We stood there.

"Oh, I see you! We're standing in line to get tickets. Can you see us?"

We both waved our hands.

"Look over to the left. No, I mean my left, your right. See us now? Hi!"

The other art girls found us, and we got on the Ferris wheel. Up on top the world was slow and dreamy, and my head filled with air. Carnival music played, bulbs were blinking. Palm trees swayed slightly before the lights of the downtown skyscrapers.

"I've got a box of copies of my book in the car, if you want to see one later."

"You wrote a book?"

"It's about falconry."

She looked at me blankly.

"It's really an extended metaphor."

"Interesting." Then quickly, delicately, after all these years, just as our car bobbed into the station, she asked:

"Who are your influences?"

"Where should I begin?" My mind raced with a list of the literary masters. I didn't just want to blurt something out, but rather structure my response to make it clear that I stood to accept the baton from the greats.

"Step to your left!" hollered the conductor, ushering us out of the car. We were whisked off the platform into the crowd, and I tailed closely behind my lovely companion.

"It's hard to say, Stella, because really I trace the form of my work to the American Moderns, but certainly the thematic content goes back much further."

"Goddamnit. We lost them again." She whipped out her phone and talked to someone, then hung up.

"Have you read *Fathers and Sons*?"

"We're meeting at a bar around the corner. I guess you can come if you want."

Stella walked so fast I couldn't continue my response. At the bar, ranchera music played and the tables were empty. The girls smoked at the booth with a man in a brown suit and a thin mustache I'd seen earlier at the gallery. I could tell right off that he was tagging along with the girls and not really wanted, and luck would have it that the only seat left for me was beside him. I decided to ignore him. We or-

dered beer and it wasn't very loud and I had all night to tell
the ladies about Knut Hamsun.

"Are you getting service in here?" said Ophelia, pushing
buttons on her phone.

"No, are you?"

"I'll go outside to the pay phone."

But the pay phone was broken so they stacked all the
phones on the table and we looked at them glumly. Nobody
spoke.

"Why don't you two talk about writing?" Stella said
suddenly to me and the man in the suit. "You're both writers, aren't you?"

"I do declare," said the man, extending his hand. "We
have yet to be formally introduced. My name is Quentin
Coldfield."

"Travis LaFrance." I had hoped Stella would listen to
me talk, but she'd gone back to fiddling with her tele-
phone.

"About what do you write?" said Quentin in a Southern
drawl that sounded fake.

"Adventure. Violence. Love. I'm on my way to Mexico
and Spain to do a book on bullfighting."

"Dear me. So virile."

"What do you write about?"

"The sins of our forefathers. The legacy of slavery and
miscegenation with the Negro. Family secrets and family
tragedy. I'm writing a memoir about a Southern writer who
comes to Hollywood to do screenplays."

"Where are you from?"

"San Diego. But in the book I'm from Mississippi."

What a fraud. No wonder these girls don't want him

around. I didn't see how anyone so blatantly trying to copy William Faulkner could take himself seriously.

Then a phone rang. It was hard to tell which one it was. Turned out to be Quentin Coldfield's, and he picked up and murmured into it. I asked out loud whose party we were trying to get to, and no one answered, then Stella whispered to me:

"Beck's."

"Oh, Beck," I said.

"It's a right good thing I wore my Sunday finest," said Quentin Coldfield, hanging up the phone. "Elena says everybody is in formal attire."

No wonder they put up with him: He was their ticket to the party.

"Can we go like this?" said Stella.

"I think we should run home and change."

"Or at least brush our hair."

"Is Elena still wearing that dress, Quentin?"

"She neglected to mention," he said smugly.

"What about Emil? He had on, like: a T-shirt."

"We'll just stop by my house real quick."

"When's she going to call back?"

"Soon," said the Southerner.

"Let's call Mona, but tell her not to tell everyone else. We have to keep it small."

We looked at the phones on the table for a long time without talking. Stella wasn't getting service and said she might go wait on the street for the phone to ring. I felt it all slipping away. This quiet bar, this table, these slim-hipped girls I deserved in my court, asking me about the Russians, they were all on their way to the rock singer's birthday party. It wasn't fair.

"I saw him about five years ago and got his autograph for my little brother," said Esmerelda. "He's definitely hot."

"I think he's adorable."

"My hairstylist says he's totally down to earth."

"I'm getting service now."

"Let's call Elena."

"OK."

"She's not picking up."

"Let's try Emil."

"Emil's more levelheaded."

"He's not picking up, either."

"They'll call soon."

"I feel claustrophobic in here," said Esmerelda. "It's making me sleepy."

Then Quentin's phone rang again: They were to drive to a parking lot and a shuttle van would deliver us to Beck's house. Ophelia said we'd stop by her house just for a minute to freshen up. The girls stood in their high-heeled sandals. I still hadn't told them about my influences.

Travis LaFrance was being railroaded by an actual famous person. It's one thing for a good-looking chick to sneak into a rock star's birthday, but a grown man does not tag along with the pretty girls to the rock star's house. It's beneath Travis LaFrance. He didn't want to meet a famous person: He was one.

"Forget this," I said to Quentin Coldfield. "I'm not going."

I said good-bye and stomped out onto the street, slammed the car doors and squealed away. I smacked the dashboard. I'd gotten so close, but now the slim-hipped girls with the cell phones were on their way to Beck's house with a phony writer in a fake suit, but I didn't complain that Los Angeles was a shallow city or that people were stupid, but instead I thought hard about the day when girls with heart-shaped sunglasses would sneak into my own birthday party. They were dreaming just like me, and the problem, the reason things had fallen apart, it wasn't them: It was me.

I wasn't famous enough.

I spent the night at Mom and Dad's house. As with most serious artists, my parents are a prime source of embarrassment. Holding the belief that raising children requires talking to them, my parents have over the years forced me into conversations about my upbringing. They want me to tell them what they did well and what they did poorly. The question smacks of annoying California families that go to therapy together and call the parents by their first names, but I humor them with a response. I'm not mean enough to discuss their major failings, which I outlined earlier, so I usually just browbeat Dad for forcing me to play Little League when adulthood has proven that I should have just quit.

At age twelve, in my final year of Little League, the year of glory that would propel me to the third basemen slot for the Los Angeles Dodgers, my ambitions were snuffed when I failed to be drafted to the majors and was instead expected to don the hideously bright orange uniform of the minor league Orioles, a costume as dignified as county jail coveralls, and to play the season with nine- and ten-year-olds instead of my sixth-grade classmates. On Cap Night, when the teams were announced, when my friends were getting their major league caps, I flung mine at the asphalt and announced to Dad that I quit. Somehow he coerced me into continuing, hinting that maybe I'd be drafted up mid-season, a rare but not impossible event when someone in the majors moved away or died. But I was never drafted. I spent the entire season in ridiculous orange, even in the end-of-year twelve-year-olds' game, in which everyone on the diamond wore major league uniforms except for me and two girls who, like me, were actually excellent players.

Dad is eager to learn from his errors, and so on the eve of my plane flight, when I told my parents that I'd already had to scrap the *Toro* proposal and plunge willy-nilly into a city larger than New York and Los Angeles combined, he made an excellent suggestion:

"Is it too late to back out?"

Yes, it was too late to back out. I'd already spent most of the book advance on back rent and the plane ticket. My mother tried to encourage me, assuring me I'd find a good story down there if I kept plugging away. Understand that my mother's advice is always suspect. Although she has lived in Los Angeles for thirty-five years, she maintains the accent she brought out West from her hometown in South Carolina where the streets are named after her ancestors. And though she holds several college degrees and once marched for civil rights, she retains some ideas from her Baptist upbringing that might be called archaic. She believes rapists should be castrated, welfare mothers sterilized after the third baby, and murderers and child molesters "put on an island."

"What was it that made Hemingway so good?" she asked me. She begins this way because she certainly doesn't remember the story and, come to think of it, probably never read the book. "Didn't he write about bullfighting in Mexico?"

"That was Spain."

"Are you sure?"

"The only book Hemingway wrote about Mexico was *The Old Man and the Sea*."

"What was that about?"

"You remember," I said patiently. "The old man who finds the biggest pearl the village has ever seen. He thinks it will solve all his problems, but instead it just makes everyone else jealous, and ruins his life, so finally he hurls it back to the sea."

"That's depressing."

"Hemingway never apologized, and I won't do it for him."

"I remember reading a book of his about bullfighting when I was in Europe," said Dad. "Must have been forty years ago."

"*Death in the Afternoon?*"

"I think it was called *Fiesta*. Does that sound right?"

"Never heard of it. He didn't write it."

"Maybe it was *This Side of Paradise*," said Mom.

"That's about Italy. Dad must be thinking of *The Sun Also Rises*."

"Is that where he falls in love with the nurse?" asked Mom.

"Ashley Brett. His greatest heroine. She and Jake Barnes go to Spain to join Franco's army and fight the Republicans, but she ends up running off with a bullfighter."

"Wasn't he friends with the matador?"

"An acquaintance."

"And they both loved Ashley Brett?"

"But she couldn't stay with Jake because of his old bull-fighting wound."

"What you need to do," exclaimed Mom, "is go down there and steal a woman away from one of these guys!"

Dad cut in. "I wouldn't get between a bullfighter and his woman."

"I was only joking," said Mom.

"It's asking for trouble," said Dad. "You just never know."

These are the conversations, I lamented, that drive a writer into exile. How can my parents understand that with each word they isolate me and my aesthetic further from the morass of throwaway American culture? But if it's exile they want, exile they shall have, and I saw that in exile I could join the other greats who in a foreign country distilled their art into its purest form. So I did not despair at my parents' house, because I knew that in the morning I'd board an AeroMexico jet for the largest city in the world, where not a single soul knew who I was or who I wasn't. This time tomorrow I'd no longer be lecturing my ignorant parents at the dinner table but, armed with a high school Spanish vocabulary and a handy list of bullfighting terms, I'd deplane in Mexico City as the incomparable Travis LaFrance, and even if I didn't find the burro and blanket and empty desert sky, tomorrow would begin a new chapter, one that my biographer, if he understands the power of simple phrases, will surely title "Expatriate: The Mexican Era."

CHAPTER FOUR

———

FREEDOM AT LAST. AS THE JET LIFTED UP OVER Los Angeles I recalled Travis's love for flight and his kinship with the falcon. He dabbles in parachuting, hang gliding, and twin-engine Cessnas, and never feels so free as when he defeats the gravity that chains him to the earth. Myself, I'm terrified of airplanes. On the runway I sat in my seat forcing a look of calm, when actually I was imagining in great detail the chain of events it would take to notify my family of my demise when the wing falls off and we plummet to the sea. Which is not to say I know nothing about falconry. I read quite a few books on the subject, and even attended a number of bird-club outings while researching the column that became my first book. But a short history of my literary career thus far reveals that while Travis certainly inspires me toward passions and dangers of the flesh, I am principally a wordsmith.

Fun with Falconry sprang from the most swashbuckling magazine to click through the copy machine in years. *Western Dude* reported dune-buggy excursions, lost treasure digs, and sea-monster hunts, those mustache-and-Schlitz adventures whose dignity had been shadowed and popularity eclipsed by the noxious cloud of such televised child's

play as wakeboarding and skysurfing and loop-de-loop bicy-
cle jumping. Leave the gadgets and soda pop sponsorships
to the kids; the men will be hunkered down in the desert
rubbing two sticks together to light a cigarette.

Using my nom de guerre, I dialed the New York publishing firms on a crusade not just to entice advertisers but
to save the book business from its stagnant irrelevance. If
they just took a minute to read about a Sasquatch sighting in San Bernardino or a collapsed mineshaft in Trona
they'd surely buy a full page. Attention, Random House:
Travis LaFrance is calling and he means to put the back-
bone back in books!

But no publisher ever bought an ad. The assistant
message-taker at the parent corporation told me to submit
something called a media kit. You'd assume this thin-
blooded lackey had chosen his career to mingle with actual
writers, but in a sad twist, on the occasions when calls came
from Travis LaFrance—nimble resuscitator of the written
word, sportsman and author in the mold of Ivan Turgenev—
the phone jockey always had more important papers to shuf-
fle or pie charts to stencil. He exiled our hero to the darkest
recesses of the voice mail labyrinth, a dungeon so despair-
ingly Byzantine that on the occasion when I surfaced to a
bored publicist confessing to feeling "cool" reading her
comped copy of *Dude* on the subway, I felt I'd scored not just
a laurel for the daredevil aesthetic, but also a minor triumph
for the arts and letters in general.

Western Dude marched along proudly, ignored by the
keepers of the canon and swindled by our so-called distrib-
utors—the malevolent alliance of hooded executioners in
warehouses who hacked off our precious covers and shipped
the corpses to the recyclery and the faceless cubicloids who

wrote sneering little checks for thirty-six dollars after we'd shipped three hundred copies. We could no longer deny that our work was simply too bold for the contemporary public. And just as we rented a storage unit to hoard boxes of unsold copies until they became collectible, there came a break in the fog of ignorance that had socked in New York for half a decade, and someone made an offer on *Fun with Falconry*.

Acclaim, long past due, was on the way. The publisher was independent enough to take a chance on a rogue like LaFrance, and the advance was small enough to let me fashion Travis as an underappreciated literary outsider. A young David unwilling to genuflect before corporate Goliath, LaFrance would prove that real writers spring from the American soil, not the skyscrapers of New York, and they'd recognize him pronto as young Turgenev with a falcon on his shoulder and say it's about time someone swept the dust off *A Hunter's Notebook*: We've waited a hundred and fifty years! The editor envisioned a Falcon 2000 promotional tour from Los Angeles to Tucson to Albuquerque to Denver to Salt Lake to Seattle to Portland to San Francisco, and I scheduled time off from the boatyard to travel the land and meet face-to-face with Travis's readers.

And just as I had finished crafting the press blurbs depicting Travis as an indie rebel, the editor called to say that our publisher had been bought by the sixth-richest man in the world, whose business dabblings beyond book publishing included Fox Television and the Los Angeles Dodgers, to name just a few. And quickly I saw that Travis LaFrance's contributions to the American canon simply could not be restricted to the margins of literature, and that his overriding vision is to unite his readers, not divide them. Having a multinational conglomerate behind *Falconry* would in fact make it easier for the Common Man to buy a copy, and wouldn't that ultimately increase the universality of its themes? What's more, as a kid I had dreamed of playing for the Dodgers, preferably third base, and I might have succeeded, if not for my parents' cutting short my fourth-grade season, in which I was leading the league in batting average, and taking me to goddamned Papua New Guinea. In a sense, with the new publisher now here I was playing for the same team as _____ and _____, the most recent Dodger stars—I have to admit I don't know their names. I stopped paying attention about 1982 after the team lost its personality, the same year incidentally that I failed to be drafted from the Little League minors to the majors. The point being: I now saw that the great thing about corporate mergers and globalization was how they let us feel that, in a way, we all play for the same team.

But for all my new coach's power, he couldn't prevent some unfortunate misunderstandings once *Fun with Falconry* reached the reviewers. I'm still convinced critics liked the book more than they let on. Even the fellow who gave it an eighth-of-a-page trouncing in *The New York Times* did so not with malice, but with the best of intentions. Circumstances prove that he was not such a bad guy.

Though certainly an accomplished author, the reviewer was foremost an exclusive hairdresser who coifed Manhattan's most famous heads. Under the pen name Newton "Knuckles" Babette, he had written a pair of semi-autobiographical detective books about an Upper East Side salon owner who moonlighted as a tough-talking private eye. If you have read *Curl Up and Dye* or *The Sharpest Scissor*— I was unable to locate copies as, sadly, both mysteries are out of print—you know that Knuckles Babette is a real hard case who doesn't take crap from anyone and smashes the stereotype of effeminate and obsequious hairdressers. In an interview I read in *Vogue,* the author revealed that he created Knuckles because he was sick of people thinking him a pantywaist just because he cut hair and fingernails for a living.

But Babette's career didn't really flourish until he gave up whodunits and wrote a sensational tell-all about New York's fanciest beauty parlors. After reading *Behind the Permed Curtain* you will always raise an eyebrow when your hair man excuses himself to that little closet by the rest room to get a refill on "product." The book was a blockbuster, and Knuckles Babette is now renowned as the chain-smokinest, whiskey-shootinest, ass-kickinest, rock-n-rollinest hairdresser this side of Paris, as red-blooded and macho as any construction worker or firefighter.

Unfortunately, when Babette reviewed *Falconry,* his exposé hadn't yet gone huge. He was still just a frustrated middle-aged manicurist with a couple of failed books, and stumbling upon Travis LaFrance's electrifying prose and devilish masculinity, he was apparently overcome with envy. He masked his admiration with pokes and backhanded compliments that to the uninformed reader may have seemed petty or snide, or even raised an alarm that the noble tradition of balanced literary review had digressed into a mine-is-bigger-than-yours cockfight. "When LaFrance's falcons flap laboriously into the ill-rendered sunset," wrote Babette, "this reader will be quite content if they never return to the hutch."

But I knew that Knuckles Babette meant no harm. If he thinks that creating a robust literary alter ego will somehow bolster his own suspect masculinity, he deserves our pity, not scorn. Even a vigorous outdoorsman and falconer such as myself, tormented by this society's high standards for manhood, sometimes doubts his own machismo, and I assume that for a hairdresser it must be even worse. So I don't begrudge Babette for those kicks to the ribs of Travis LaFrance. Even though each blow hurt deeply, right to the kidneys, Travis understood that lying there and taking the boots was helping Knuckles work through some issues. Travis and I were honored to do it, sure Babette would return the favor to a fellow writer in need. Under different circumstances, I think my persona and his persona would be regular pals, and if I ever make it to New York I'll march right into his salon with a six-pack of beer and belly up to the bar for a pedicure.

As a new member of the Twentieth Century Fox Dodgers, Travis LaFrance was quickly shipped down to the farm league. By order of the new general manager, the Falcon 2000 tour was scrapped. But the good news was that a dozen or more radio stations wanted on-the-air interviews with Travis LaFrance. I received a call from a golden-voiced East Coast deejay who administered a radio training session in which I learned that I should hold the phone directly to my mouth, speak slowly, and prepare notes to prompt myself.

"By the way," I asked my radio trainer, "do the producers who call already understand the book's multiple levels? Or will I have to explain it?"

"Oh, they don't call us. Your publisher pays us to get you these slots."

All the more incentive to impress them with the complexity of my work. So I scribbled a few ideas, four or five pages about Turgenev and Mark Twain and literature for the Common Man, trying to strike the balance between folksy and literate that would resonate with the intellectual types who listen to book shows.

"This is Jack from the Jack and Jerry Morning Show on WBFI 850 AM, Dayton's best AM drive-time talk!"

I was lying in bed cradling the phone beneath the night-light, 4:30 in the morning my time, making some final cross-outs to my appraisal of the endurance of the Russian novel.

"We'll have another traffic update in four minutes," said the deejay, "but first we've got Trevor LaFrancis live on the line from Utah and get this, folks, he's written a book about birds!"

I cleared my throat patiently.

"The book is about birds only insomuch as the falcons serve as a metaphor for my flight toward freedom, both personally and artistically."

"Whatever you say, dude. Now, can you train one of those buggers to attack somebody?"

"I volunteer my ex-wife," said his sidekick, and a bell in the studio went *ding-dong ding-dong*.

So successful was my radio debut that Falcon 2000 revived on a scale less ostentatious than the previously planned national tour. Instead of spreading my talent thin in the big cities, I'd go straight to the heartland for a single and singular event at Barnes & Noble in Orem, Utah. Orem sits beside Brigham Young University, stronghold of the Mormon kingdom, and driving up from Moab in the afternoon, I debated which chapter to read. I didn't want to

offend the locals with yarns of petty crime and drunk driving and underage girls, topics I understood to be more
gritty and therefore literary, which I would guard in my
docket for more urbane audiences down the line. So I chose
a chapter that everyone could enjoy, even the kids, especially the kids. When Travis LaFrance says he writes for the
people, he means all the people.

Surprise me, Orem! Put yourself on the map! Make yourself remembered as the literary weathervane, disguised as
any other strip-mall suburb, that lit the fuse of the *Falconry*
explosion.

My main concern was that the store would run out of
books. The buzz about *Falconry* that had so successfully
eluded the media had likely gone straight to the people,
and there could be a mob of fans to see me. I had packed a
carton of four dozen books in the back of the truck, just in
case.

I found the store in the same plaza as MacFrugal's and
Ross Dress for Less and mused that literature finds the
strangest bedfellows. I left my dog with a water bowl in the
truck, and went inside. There in the entrance stood a sign
with my picture and the book cover. Already I could tell
this was going to be big. The Director of Community Relations showed me the folding chairs and couches where the
audience would gather.

"Do you want a latté or anything?" she said.

I reached for my wallet and pretended it wasn't there. I
said no thanks.

"Policy is you get one free."

First class.

"Yes, then. If you insist."

"Sugar in it?"

"Black, thanks."

She looked perplexed, apparently unaccustomed to a man who thirsts for just the essentials. When she went to fetch it I found the magazine rack and wondered what Travis LaFrance would read to perfect his image of a stoic malcontent. I finally decided on *The Nation*, to embody a blend of blue-collar politics and searing intellect. I coughed up three-fifty, reasoning that I'd be so busy signing autographs that I wouldn't finish reading it tonight. With the hour approaching, the Director of Community Relations delivered my coffee and announced over the loudspeakers that at seven sharp Travis LaFrance would be reading from *Fun with Falconry*, and with five minutes to spare she escorted me to the cookbook area, where we found all the folding chairs still empty.

"Tuesdays don't always have a big draw," said the Director of Community Relations.

But there were four readers slumped in the sofas around the folding chairs, having come early to get the good seats. They were few, but they were proud, and I loved them each, admired their resolve to defy their philistine neighbors and venture out on a Tuesday and show that Orem wasn't just some soulless grid of boulevards but a concrete bohemia. The DCR went to make a final announcement, and I watched to see how my four devotees would react. Would they look up from their books and skip a heartbeat with anticipation, or did they already sense my presence and would just play it cool? The fine thing about the early stages of stardom, I reflected, was that I could still walk freely in public without being recognized. I decided to savor this moment of anonymity as something quaint to be one day looked back upon with wistful nostalgia: Ah, the

Throngs of admiring fans are a fact of life for toreros and adventure-authors alike.

days when I could browse in a bookstore and not be hounded for autographs!

But then something strange happened. The final call came over the speakers and none of my fans looked up. Not even a shift in their seats to get a better view, not a pause from their reading to acknowledge they'd found the place. Nothing. Perhaps they were deaf. And it wasn't until the DCR returned with an apologetic look that I realized that as much as I loved the couch-sitters, they hadn't come out this Tuesday to hear Travis LaFrance. They were simply sitting on the sofas because the sofas were soft, and it was not my place to enlighten them when all they'd come for was some peaceful albeit uninspired quiet. The DCR and I traded a few glances, agreed that the nuances of LaFrance's prose would be lost on these simple people, and decided to proceed directly to the book-signing event.

I positioned myself at the table, flanked by the sign and
partially hidden by a stack of my books. People walking
through the door averted their eyes and steered clear. Just
then a folksinger started strumming his guitar in the Barnes
& Noble Café, and the DCR informed me that I was also
entitled to a free dinner. I went to the counter and ordered
a bowl of mushroom soup and a bottle of apple juice. There
was nowhere to sit, though, because the folksinger had
drawn a crowd of perky virginal coeds, and after each of
the tunes—upbeat numbers revealing that falling in love is
happy but breaking up is sad—the harem erupted into
adoring applause for their songster, a dimpled pup about
half my age with gelled hair and a winning smile.

I did not hate him. He could not understand the foolishness of his position, that his apparent triumph tonight would
be anecdotally mocked by historians as but a frivolous disservice to the budding career of Travis LaFrance. These small
indignities would only burnish the story my biographers
told. Nor did I loathe the college girls, who had entered a
sanctum where books are allegedly sold, but who could not
peel their gazes from their pop singer long enough to note
in their midst Travis LaFrance, writer of books and lover
of women. I felt grief, some pity, nothing more. Through
clenched teeth I spoke a small elegy for the written word.

Just then I looked up and was surprised to see a brave
customer at my table, thumbing through the pages. But by
the time I'd gulped down the soup and hurried back to my
station, the reader was gone. I sat down. I continued reading *The Nation*, a bit irked about blowing four bucks, and
the more I read about big business's domination of politics

and the imminent onset of a corporate monoculture, the better I understood that in manning the unpeopled *Falconry* table, I was not simply a hero, I was a martyr, literature's solitary spokesman on display like a criminal here in the mall. Might as well insert my head and feet in the stocks and dangle an AUTHOR sign from my neck, let the children gawk and pity me while the adults dart toward the cookbooks in ignorance and indifference.

On the verge of hemorrhaging with indignation, I sensed someone near and looked up from my magazine: It was my fan, the one who'd been looking at the book. She'd returned.

"I guess the open mike is canceled," she said.

I wasn't sure how to answer. She told me that usually on Tuesday nights they had poetry readings, which is why she came, but tonight they had me instead. She asked how the reading went, and I told her. She winced.

"I'm a writer, too," she said. "Sometimes I read my poems here."

"Well, good."

"And I'm an artist." The girl told me that she'd just graduated from high school in upstate New York and had moved to Utah to go to community college. It was nice not being the only Mormon, she said. She was taking some art classes now.

"What kind of art do you do?"

"I'll show you."

The girl opened a big knapsack. She said she wanted to make a postcard out of the drawing she was working on. She showed me the sketches. In the first frame, a skinny frog on a lily pad was eyeing a fly overhead. In the second, he was airborne, lunging with an elastic tongue. In the third frame the frog was back on the lily pad, fat now, smiling.

"I like it," I said.

"It'll look better once it's painted with colors. This is just a sketch."

"It's great."

So we talked about what it was like to be an artist. We had that in common. I told her that I also worked for a river company down in the desert.

"You mean you're a river guide?"

"Well, in a sense."

"I bet that's so exciting! I'd be afraid of the big rapids."

"You get used to it. By now it's second nature."

"Wow. How much does your book cost?"

"Thirteen bucks."

"Do they have it at the library?"

"I doubt it," I said. "I wish it didn't cost so much."

"Yeah," she said. "How do you know so much about falcons?"

"It's just a hobby. The book's not really about falcons."

"Why not?"

"It's more of a novel. Based on something by Turgenev."

"Is that a writer?"

"A Russian."

"That's cool," she said, "I guess."

Then in the doorway appeared a river guide I worked with in Moab. Wasn't it just like him to travel all this way to spoil my moment of acclaim? He'd probably tell my fan that I wasn't actually a river guide, or that my real name wasn't even Travis LaFrance. So I said good-bye to the fan and bolted to the nearest aisle. When my co-worker saw me browsing in the self-help books, I gave a very casual fancy-meeting-you-here type of wave and when he asked what I was doing in Orem I said, "Just looking around."

I decided, then, that LaFrance should practice some erratic behavior to stir up controversy and nurture his cult of personality. Something to get in the tabloids. Shielding my face with my magazine I snuck past the cash registers and, without telling even the Director of Community Relations, fled from the bookstore into the mini-mall traffic of a Tuesday night, leaving everyone inside to wonder what had become of the mysterious Travis LaFrance.

The next day as I raced my truck up into the mountains, I imagined the news of my disappearance in Orem spreading via phone call and e-mail—Did you hear about LaFrance's stunt last night? That man follows nobody's rules!—and soon I was light-headed with visions of being toasted at that New York bar where they always toast writers in the movies, the inevitable *Rolling Stone* interview, and finally, sweetly, the savage editorial in *The Wall Street Journal* citing the Knuckles Babette review as evidence of the falling standards and stunted vision at *The New York Times* book page. *Fun with Falconry* stuns the naysayers and claims the National Book Award. We knew it all along, cries the chorus of critics, we just didn't have the courage to speak.

Brimming with the swagger that had made *Falconry* such a gem, I turned off the main highway and up into the Huntington hills. I had the dog in the back and the windows rolled down. I'd take a small adventure. Too giddy to stop for a meal, I rolled up on a man selling beef jerky in a turnout. I felt kinship with the jerky man as he plied his craft nobly, stoically, out here in the hinterland, unrecognized by the East Coast jerkiati, but not for long, no, not for too much longer. Certain circumstances might just take a sudden upswing for Travis LaFrance and the roadside jerky man.

"Between two artisans," I told him, "how about we barter this collectible volume on falconry for a half-pound of the teriyaki?"

He handled the book, opened the cover, gave it back.

"Nine dollars a bag."

Why not? I'm Travis LaFrance, adventure writer, and I'll take two bags, thanks. Keep the change on the twenty, and keep the book, too. We're both getting a good deal here.

I drove on, the freedom of it, the beauty, the banana milkshakes and corn dogs in a burger shack in some town, just baking there in the sun, a fine uncelebrated little Utah town, proud and indifferent to the rest of the world. I raced down a green creek canyon and into the desert, already headed to the interstate when I discovered on the map a shortcut through the San Rafael Swell, a longcut actually, fifty miles of dirt road labeled "unimproved." What the hell, if the road got too rough for my two-wheel-drive truck, I could just turn around, as long as I didn't wait too long and get perched on some narrow cliff ledge or buried to the axle in a sand pit, but that wouldn't happen, and big deal if it did, I could just walk, the very farthest it could be was twenty-five miles, and if I walked all night keeping a slow but steady pace, I'd be in town before the heat got really life-threatening. What provisions did I need beside this well-crafted jerky? I'm Travis LaFrance! It's not like I was going to spend the night out there. Two hours max. I filled up two quarts of water at a gas station and headed into the desert.

The dirt road dipped into a steep-walled canyon and wound toward the San Rafael River. It was fine. This would be fine. I sped up a bit, clenching the steering wheel, keeping it safe. And passing a low-clearance rented sedan coming the other direction, I figured the road couldn't get much worse where I was headed. I reached the river, just a trickle through a bed of sand, but a brave and heroic one, spanned by a handsome one-lane bridge. Who would have thought? A bridge! Twenty-five miles from the nearest pavement, as if installed by those forward-thinking folks at the Civilian Conservation Corps with the express purpose of getting Travis LaFrance across this quicksand bog on his route to literary importance. I let the dog wade into the creek and get a sip of water, then back on the road. I knew I was through the worst of it, well-graded dirt from here to the interstate. I let the speedometer inch its way up, 35, 40, 45—nothing in the world is more exciting than driving fast on dirt roads. Seat belt? Ha! I'm the only car on the road! The dust rose up behind me, seeping through the camper shell into the cab. The dog climbed into my lap and I shut the cab window, really moving now, faster and faster, feeling the back end slide around the curves, and thinking how young and silly I'd been seven years ago when I flipped my station wagon on a road just like this, fishtailing too fast around a corner, but now I was such a better driver, I'd been doing this for years, I was a regular pro, seasoned and skilled on these desert roads, and as the interstate came into view I let out a yelp and hit the gas, home free on a straightaway, until here came the final bend, and didn't it look like a good place to fishtail, so I punched it and cranked the wheel and oh shit here we go oh fuck I knew this was going to happen spinning out of control one way now the other why am I such an idiot can't I ever learn from my past mistakes god damn off the road into the ditch and up and yes shit here it comes, yes, over.

Broken glass. A little blood.

Begin inventory. Skull: fine. Organs: fine. Limbs: bruised, cut, nothing serious. Apparently unhurt. Dog: frightened and upset but willing to forgive, reconcile. I lift her out the passenger window then climb out myself, out of my downed spacecraft into the Martian desert.

Fuck.

This sort of thing does not happen to Travis LaFrance.

The truck was on its side. I pushed it. Maybe it would flop back on its tires and I'd drive away, real quiet-like, pretending this had never happened, would never happen again. But it didn't budge.

The camper shell had wrenched off in the wreck, spilling all its contents into the dirt—tools and jumper cables and the plywood bed and a sleeping bag and, there in the midst of it, a box of books, forty-eight mint copies of *Fun with Falconry*, flung into the grit, covers torn, bindings bashed, pages filled with sand. I tried to give some dignity to the scene by arranging the debris in a neat pile, to present myself as master of this current predicament in the event someone should happen by. Once I chased down my dog, who had run off in the opposite direction, we walked together toward the interstate.

And suddenly I was happy, ecstatic, euphoric! Travis LaFrance had survived yet another auto wreck, lived through another action-packed chapter for his next book. Yes, these setbacks do befall adventure heroes, but what makes them heroes is their ability to bounce back, to get back on the horse. I sucked the blood from my fingers. I was unstoppable, with an angel looking down to protect me from disaster.

The highway on-ramp where I arrived was about halfway between Green River and Salida, that hundred-mile desert stretch without any services or towns, the longest such stretch in the lower forty-eight. I remember crossing it as a child in the heat of summer, imagining how desperate it would be to be stuck out here without water; now here I was, a twenty-nine-year-old man, stuck out here alone with a few sips left in my water bottle.

But not to worry: I was on a highway. Surely some Good Samaritan would pull off momentarily to help. I walked up the off-ramp and waved at a westbound car, whose occupants quickly pretended to be adjusting the stereo knobs. The sun was setting and a warm breeze blew. Despite my circumstances it was very pleasant. I didn't look too dangerous: My hair was short and I had a dog. Besides that I was Travis LaFrance, heir-American to the Russian novel. Someone would stop.

More cars blew past.

As soon as a car came into view, it switched lanes and blasted by at seventy-five, its driver not even looking at me. What did they think I wanted? I clearly had no luggage or possessions with me; I wasn't asking for a ride to California. Somebody do literature a favor and pick me up! I waved my arms and hopped up and down. Still not even eye contact. I screamed "Help!" but the more commotion I caused, the more I looked like a lunatic. So I was in a bind as to how to present myself, stranded there on the highway at sunset. Calm and collected? Or would that just make me seem OK, really, no big hurry to get out of here anytime soon. Frantic and victimized? That only turns people off. They don't want your problems in their car. Or maybe friendly. I could give a big smile, like: Howdy, partner, ain't it strange that we meet here, this time of night, this far from anywhere? But that's transparent and makes you seem a serial killer, trying to smile your way into range.

No. There was simply no good way to do this. I was just plain fucked, learning by the moment the real meaning of marginalized. From the other side of their speeding windshields, I was the enemy—dangerous or crazy or smelly or just too much trouble, and the more I pleaded with these assholes behind their steering wheels sipping sodas and scribbling on crossword puzzles, the more I hated them and wanted to see one go somersaulting off the highway across the sagebrush. But then, what would I do in their position, seeing some grubby loner waving his arms like a spastic? I'd stop for them, I promised myself. I'd picked up hitchhikers around here before. I'd do it again, goddamnit. When a car slowed down a bit and lowered the window, I yelled that I'd had a crash, and he yelled that he'd call for help at the next stop, then roared off, never even stopping. I wondered if he knew it was sixty miles to the next phone.

I was rescued finally by an old couple putting along the dirt road where I'd crashed, two dogs in the backseat of their Jeep. They had been excited to find my wrecked car, they told me, and seemed a bit disappointed that I had walked away from it, that they hadn't discovered my carcass slumped in the front seat. I asked them if they'd take me back to the scene and help me push the car over, and they gave each other a quiet look as though I'd proposed murder.

"You're the author," said the lady, and I gave a modest nod, flattered to be getting some recognition all the way out here in the middle of nowhere, wondering which newspaper clip they'd read about me.

"We saw your picture on the books in the dirt."

She said they'd be happy to take me up the interstate and find a highway patrolman who could help me, and by now it was almost dark, and I couldn't foresee a better option, so my dog and I squeezed in back with the other dogs, a floating sensation in my stomach, feeling things spiral out of my grasp. Highway patrol meant police report meant tow truck meant insurance company meant rate increases meant money and on and on.

As Falcon 2000 ground to a halt, I was out one truck and about one hundred dollars in travel expenses. I'd sold three books and destroyed fifty. Travis LaFrance felt the clippers pressed cold beneath his wings, and it wasn't until months later when he boarded that jet for Mexico City that once again he extended those wings and soared.

CHAPTER FIVE

———

"MY ART IS MY LIFE, AND VERSA VICE," SAYS Travis LaFrance more than once in the pages of *Toro,* coining what will likely become the mantra of his generation. He is the envy of every man who has aspired to live by a code of courage and beauty: He walks the soil shooting tequila and bedding maidens and tempting death, then writes it all down and cashes the checks. And just as the artist must spread the paint and the matador must court the bull, in order to answer his creative calling Travis LaFrance must always feel on his wrist the lacy fingers of a daring and exotic female.

How does he find them? Travis LaFrance doesn't comb the bars making passes and stammering for small talk, and never ends up listening to someone drone on about her dumb marketing job and dull jealous boyfriend. The women simply appear at the beginning of each chapter, already aware of his reputation and smitten by his rugged charm, ready to leap into amorous adventure. Look at Victoria the tragic heiress and Carmen the teenage bullfighter; remember Latecia the flamenco dancer and Hannah Kjoprczak the dissident photojournalist. *Toro* is a page-turning pageant of this hemisphere's most memorable ladies.

Although it's Travis LaFrance who seduces these lovelies, I will humbly take credit for recruiting them. I went to Mexico not for bullfights, but for women, to irrigate the narrative with a steady flow of romance. And though searching the bars and beaches of Mexico bravely courting girls was not my idea of a good time, I did it, reader, for you. I even came to enjoy the work. In picking women to appear in a timeless work of art, in matchmaking for eternity with literature's most eligible cocksman, I was doing them a service. Surely I wouldn't have refused a kiss now and then, and yes, I had my share of daydreams while penning the steamy bedroom scenes, but my motives for what might have appeared simple womanizing were, believe me, strictly literary.

Touching down in Mexico City on a Friday evening, I calculated that before the Sunday corrida I had forty hours to snare a love interest. Maybe it would be easy. The hotel would likely be ripe with supple bachelorettes.

A forty-dollar taxi ride delivered me to a ten-dollar downtown hotel, and I carried my bags to the third floor, where a bruised mattress lay flat on bare tile. There was plenty of water in the shower and it was all cold. The other tenants I saw were Mexican families with small children. I figured the fashionable ladies were already out for the evening. I lay on the bed, dazed, wondering what time zone I was in.

Then I realized that except for the deskman who'd looked at my passport, nobody in this country knew my name, and as far as they could tell, I wasn't just the man behind LaFrance, I was Travis himself. So I went outside to test out my new identity. The boulevard traffic never stopped, and walking on the blackened sidewalks was like inhaling through an exhaust pipe. Travis would earn his true grit in this city. Some people wore surgeon's masks and bandannas over their mouths, but I decided to toughen up and gulped up the smog thirstily. After a few blocks, my eyes watered and stung, and I coughed like I'd smoked a full pack.

Nobody came right out and asked my name, but I felt a new reverence in the looks of strangers. I sat alone in a concrete diner and the waitress could tell I was someone important, because instead of what I ordered, she served up a svelte drumstick in red sauce that must have been the house special. Just yesterday I might have sent it back and had them cook it more, but now as Travis LaFrance I savored the blue veins in the pink meat as an exotic delicacy. I went back to the hotel to peruse the lobby for young ladies, only to discover that there was no lobby. I lay down in my room. A fluorescent light burned through the window, and people and children were clacking on the courtyard floor and yapping until morning.

The next day I called a phone number I'd procured my night in Echo Park. When I told Stella I was going to Mexico City, she'd given me the name of someone she knew. I was relieved when the person who answered spoke English, and after I explained who gave me his name, I said my name was Travis LaFrance.

"I'm Miguel."

"The writer," I added.

"You can come over if you want. I'm not really doing anything."

When the taxi dropped me, I was introduced to two more people whose names I promptly forgot, then we loaded into a small sedan and drove off. Miguel asked if I'd rather go to a movie or a party, and I said a party. Ninety seconds later, we stopped on the sidewalk and he asked if I would like to sit in front. Miguel went into a restaurant, I took his seat, and we sped off.

"Where am I going?" I said to the woman driving.

A party.

"Where's Miguel?"

A movie. She drove dangerously through the streets, discussing with the other passenger in a fast, indecipherable dialect how to get where we were going. "In Mexico you can drive anyway you want," she told me in English, making a U-turn on a freeway on-ramp.

"What language are you two speaking?"

"Spanish."

"Oh."

"We're from Uruguay. That's why you can't understand us."

Soon we arrived at a swank apartment, were buzzed through the door, and found ourselves at a dinner party of Uruguayans, Colombians, Spaniards, and Mexicans, all of whom seemed to descend from royalty and now worked in advertising. A television showed MTV with Spanish subtitles, and the stereo console housed green bars of lights that bumped up and down in time to the music. The advertisers talked about bus versus metro, safe neighborhoods, taxis, and good Italian restaurants. These were not the sunbeaten campesinos I had proposed to write about, and I could understand only parts of what they said, so I tuned out. If I couldn't go home and write it down in my book, there was no sense in listening.

In walked a woman so proud and striking that she must have been a countess or a movie star, someone whose love life and wardrobe you read about at the checkout aisle. She was shrink-wrapped in white flares and a maroon leather coat, dancing across the room kissing cheeks and singing, "Soy Victoria! Mucho gusto! Soy Victoria!" She flicked away her coat, revealing lovely freckled shoulders beneath the strings of a halter top, then sat cross-legged on a pillow and lit a cigarette. Her voice quivered with an aristocratic Spanish lisp; then, upon learning that I was American, she broke into the Queen's English. Her father was British, she said, her mother Mexican, and she was raised in Madrid. Amid screams of laughter she announced that she was entirely crazy and she certainly didn't have a boyfriend.

The British accent, the streaks of blond, the form-fitting slacks—I had found a woman just like Hemingway's Ashley Brett. In an instant I sketched out Travis's first bittersweet affair in the book: the wide-brimmed hat she'd wear in the plaza de toros, the way I'd shield her eyes when the blood pulsed from the bull, the late nights of martinis and sharp banter, the way she'd cry "Bung-o!" or "Bother!" whenever she felt a breakdown coming. I pictured us flying together first class somewhere and checking into the Ritz, wherever that is. And when I asked if she'd be going to the corrida the next day, she remembered she had a polo match to attend instead.

I had arrived! Though technically I hadn't asked her out, I proudly claimed her reply as a dignified No-thank-you, so far above the dismissals I was accustomed to, the No-I-have-to-work and the No-I'm-going-to-a-movie, and the No-I-have-a-boyfriend. A polo match! I thought polo only happened in movies. It was one step short of No-I'm-jetting-to-Monaco-for-tea-with-the-prince. But suddenly my Lady Victoria cocked her lovely head and addressed me loudly in English.

"If you're writing about bullfighting, you must go to Spain."

I explained that of course I would go to Spain, but first wouldn't it be fascinating to examine a New World mutation of an Old World tradition, because after all, aren't all us Americans, excuse me, we Americans . . .

"That's silly!" she snapped. "That's like coming to Mexico to write a book about"—she snorted as if dislodging the words from the back of her throat, then frowned and spat them my way—"American football."

"You're right." I was glad someone appreciated the challenge of my task and could articulate it in my own language. She did seem a bit snippy about it, but I recognized that as flirting.

"How do you know so much about bullfighting anyway?"

"I've read quite a few books."

"And how many bullfights have you been to?"

"Well, none. Yet. Not in person."

She glared at me. Everyone else had stopped talking to watch us.

"I think that's absolutely ridiculous," she hissed.

The room waited for my comeback.

"Touché," I said.

"What did you read at the university?" she demanded.

"Excuse me?"

"What did you read? Oh, what's the word? Study! That's it. What did you study at the university."

"Um, English."

"Literature," she corrected me. "I took the level A in Barcelona. And my father studied literature at Oxford. He's a writer. That's what he does. A writer. He writes, what do you call them, movie scripts. They brought him out to Hollywood."

She definitely liked me.

"He hated Hollywood. Now he's upper level at the BBC. In New York."

Even the people who didn't understand English could tell she was having a small fit of infatuation. I raised an eyebrow for the onlookers and gave my best whoop-de-fucking-do-like-I'm-really-impressed look. And instantly I was euphoric, because I knew when it came time to write this part of the book, I'd redo it with a bullish Travis LaFrance:

> "What did you read at the university?"
> "I didn't go to the university."
> "My father has a degree from Oxford."
> "Never heard of it."
> "He's an executive at the BBC."
> "What's the BCB?" snaps Travis LaFrance. "My dad's a cop."

A less-experienced ladies' man might have missed Victoria's clues. If not for my insights into the female psyche, I might have even mistaken her flirting for attempts to belittle me. Sometimes you have to let a woman feel she has the upper hand. After failing to win me over with the bullfighting tirade, she finally got so desperate for my affection that she began making fun of my ninety-peso hotel room.

"Well, I hope you didn't *want* anything you left in the room," she said with a giggle, "because *surely* it's not there anymore."

"You don't frighten me," I said. "I put everything in the safe."

"The safe!" she cried, and the others joined the laughter. "He's left it all in the safe! Darling, the robbers are the very people with the *key* to the safe!"

She then declared that I was blushing, which made me blush more. I realized that with a kicked feeling in my stomach, yes, of course, how stupid had I been, everything I owned, passport, traveler's checks, cash, it was all gone.

"Let's all go to the other party," sang Victoria, "unless the Americano needs to get back to his room at the Sheraton."

Laugh now, thought Travis LaFrance. Vengeance will come.

With everyone needing a ride, there was no room for me in the sedan, but the Uruguayans offered kindly to pop the trunk and let me sit in there. It wasn't too far of a drive. We shuttled to a fancy colonial house with red walls and orange carpets where the women laughed like music and the men wore suits and knew how to dance. I spent the hours sharpening barbed yet affectionate arrows to fling toward Victoria, but meanwhile the Lady was busy sucking down gin fizzes and doing the rumba with all the boys. Finally I got anxious, wanting to return to the hotel and check my belongings. There was no reason to rush with Victoria: It was Travis's first night out in Mexico City, and he'd get another chance to carry her back to his suite.

I decided to end the evening with a malicious zinger she could wrestle with until our next encounter, just the way Travis would do it. Once I'd figured out how this scene would end in the book, I couldn't settle for fiction. I had to act it out, which would allow me to write about what had really happened. Just before leaving I cornered Lady Victoria and peppered her with questions. She revealed that she worked for the same ad firm as the others.

"What do you do *there*?" I said.

Planning and strategy, she said. Travis smelled blood.

"What does *that* entail?" I sniffed.

Blah blah blah, she said, something about brands and television and international exposure. I cut her off mid-sentence.

"Have you *planned* any good *strategies* lately?"

Blah blah blah, she continued. I craned my neck to stare obviously at some other girl's butt. Oh, but I was enjoying myself! Travis LaFrance was the one traipsing the globe with a book contract, she was the one who sat in a cubicle all day. Analysis, sales, markets—she said more words, and I let her go on, blah blah blah, then abruptly I checked my watch, stood up, and said it was time to go. Travis LaFrance stomped off and left the lady thirsting for more.

CHAPTER SIX

I KNEW HOW TRAVIS WOULD RESPOND TO HIS
first bullfight. During the preliminaries when the woman
on his arm cringed at the spilled blood, he'd pull her close
and assure her that she was watching more than a cruel
killing. This was art. He'd explain the difference between a
rejoneador and a picador, between a novillero and a banderillero. He'd tell her when to wave her handkerchief,
when to cheer and when to whistle, and when to fling a
rose to the triumphant matador.

"Americano," says a stranger sitting beside him, "you
are not like your countrymen. How is it you comprehend
our fiesta so well?"

"My country is the whole world," says Travis.

Unlike a football fan who can just sit there and holler
like an idiot, an aficionado is expected to know something.
So before leaving California I photocopied the thirty-four-
page glossary of terms from *Death in the Afternoon*, which I
planned to carry with me at all times to distinguish myself
as a true aficionado and not just another dim gringo.

Finally the day arrives for me to prove my courage in
the bleachers. On Sunday the streets around Plaza Mexico
are cordoned off, and the taco vendors fry chunks of carni-

tas in iron cauldrons beneath shade tents. I line up with the thousands of fans at the gate to the stadium. Here I am at the largest bullring in the world, where more than fifty thousand souls shout Olé in concert, where the flame of tradition burns bright.

"Usted es aficionado?" I say to the man in front of me.

He looks at me, and at the ticket I hold in my hand.

"No is bulls here, friend. Here is fútbol." Then he points across the street. "There is bulls. Allá."

I thank him and backtrack through the crowd and across the street. Now I'm in the right place. Look at the bronze statues of bullfighters, the glorious oil-paint posters glued to the walls, but wait a minute, what's this graffiti someone has spray-painted on the temple:

Toros si, toreros no!
La tortura no es arte ni cultura
Todos toreros deben morir

Consulting my dictionary, I decipher these to be the misinformed rants of an ignoramus unable to appreciate la fiesta brava. Probably written by an American.

There is no line to enter Plaza Mexico; maybe like me everyone bought tickets the day before. I present my ticket and get a red carnation from the girls in sleeveless dresses who usher me through the portals to my seat in the shade. Down below there it is, finally: the bullring. It's blissful and holy the way Dodger Stadium used to be before an evening game in the summer, the red dirt raked to perfection, the rings of chalk as bold and sharp as if drawn with God's protractor.

But where is everyone? A machine-gunner could empty a magazine into the stands without casualties. All those

Hostesses at Plaza Mexico relish the opportunity to escort a legendary aficionado such as Travis LaFrance to his seat.

thousands of fans went to the soccer game instead. Where are the fancy socialites and hip bachelors sipping martinis? Where are the poets and painters and bohemians? Instead, fat guys in windbreakers are smoking cigars and sucking wine from leather bags. Dudes in white smocks climb the aisles selling foam cups of beer and doughnuts and hot dogs. The cheap sunny seats are separated from the shady side by a barbed-wire barricade in the style of the Tijuana border.

Then a band of old men in shirtsleeves and straw hats raise their trumpets and trombones to play a Spanish march. It's just as I had imagined it would be, until a jumbo jet roars overhead and drowns out the music. Down in the ring the gate to the tunnel swings open, and out march the bullfighters in a phalanx of snug glittery knickers and jackets, neckties and pigtails. They tip their hats. Each has an arm slung in a cape like a wounded soldier marching back from the front, complemented by bedroom slippers and surprisingly pink stockings that Travis LaFrance recognizes as part of a manly tradition, but that an uninformed American might just call fruity.

Enough of this casual observation. I reach in my pocket for my glossary of terms so that I can get down to some real appreciation.

But it's not there.

I check the other pocket. Nothing. I think back to the morning at the hotel. I had been overjoyed to discover that, contrary to Lady Victoria's prediction, nothing had been stolen. And as I had scripted the bon mots with which I'd upbraid her at our next encounter, I must have left my cheat sheet with my passport. Now I'm in trouble.

Before I can think what to do, the bull charges out of the chute into the ring lunging at anything that moves. The bullfighters shake their pink and yellow capes, then sneak behind little barriers, and the bull rams the walls, moaning and slobbering. What's going on? It looks like just a bunch of guys in sparkling suits getting chased by a bull. Suddenly the bull stops charging and people boo and whistle, but I can't figure out why, and finally the bullfighters come out and try to chase the bull back into the tunnel, and since of course they don't have lassos or cattle prods, it takes a long time. But why is the bull leaving? I don't remember from my notes.

Now a new bull charges into the ring, and two guys trot out on horseback, done up like Tweedledee and Tweedledum with their guts flopping onto the saddle and a clunky tin boot on one foot. Who are these people? They've got the horse dressed like a bed, quilt and mattress included, pillowcase over the head so it can't see a thing. Tweedledee leans toward the charging bull and sinks a lance between its shoulders, and everyone screams and boos, but I can't tell if they're mad at the bull or at the rider. How could I be so stupid as to forget my notes? I'm blowing it. I open my wallet and sort through receipts and maps but still can't find my glossary.

Blood pulses out of that wound and explodes in little splats on the sand, the reddest red I've ever seen.

Holy Shit. I shudder. Those men are actually going to kill that bull.

Now the bull scoops up the horse and rider like a fork-lift, pins them against the wall, and topples them onto the dirt. The crowd shrieks, and by the sound of it they believe that Tweedledee deserves the trampling he's getting, so I open my mouth and holler some meaningless syllables along with them.

With a fanfare of trumpets Tweedledee and Tweedle-dum limp away. There are so many guys in pink socks that I don't know who is who. One of them trades his cape for a pair of sticks wrapped in colored paper, which from where I sit look like something a clown would bring to a birthday party. He squares off against the bull, arches like a swan, and flicks his hips. They charge each other, and just as Pink-Socks is about to get a horn in the gut, he flaps his wings and launches and tries to sink the sticks in the bull's back, but they both fall out. The crowd howls, and a drunk yells an obscenity that even I understand.

The trumpet blows and the matador unveils his sword and red cape. This must be the part where we're supposed to yell Olé. That much I remember. The vendors of Domino's

Pizza sit down and stop barking. By now the bull knows
something is wrong—his sides are dripping blood, a quiver
of arrows are stuck in his back, his tongue lolls from his
mouth, and he's making moo noises. Mátale, mátale, shouts
the crowd, and I hope they're telling the authorities to call
this whole thing off before it's too late, but my dictionary
tells me they're saying kill it. And the matador makes his
passes, but instead of the crowd shouting a grand Olé, they
heckle and spit, and laugh when the torero gets tossed over
the horns.

The matador points his sword straight ahead and
arches his back. It's quiet except for the jet plane in the sky.
Is there anything I can do to stop it? I've read in books that
a perfect plunge will cut the aorta, dropping the bull instantly. I cover my eyes and wait.

The crowd groans, flips open programs, and starts talking. "Cerveza! Cerveza!" shouts the vendor. I peek through
the fingers; the bloody sword is lying in the dirt and the
bull is still on its feet. The matador picks up his weapon
and makes another stab, which goes halfway in, and then
like a waiter who's botched a wine cork he calls over the
other Pink-Socks to help. They run the bleeding bull in circles until the sword falls out, and again he stabs halfway,
and this time it won't dislodge, so someone brings a second sword and, inserting it through the handle, he extracts
the first from the bull's shoulders.

The popsicle trays come marching down the aisle. The
bull collects more stab wounds. The last words he will hear
on this planet will be a sales pitch for a twenty-five-peso
Personal Pizza. Delicioso! Caliente! Down in the dirt they
keep stabbing the bull, and I remember the time my
brother and I shot a squirrel with our single-pump Red Ry-

der BB gun, knocking it off a branch, but after numerous point-blank shots to the head realized we lacked the firepower to do the job right, then scrambled to find a big rock and finally crushed the critter's skull in a ceremony slightly more graceful than the spectacle before me in the Plaza Mexico. By the time the bull finally crumples to the dirt the crowd is irate. People frisbee their seat cushions down at the Pink-Socks. Maybe they're going to call this thing off. I look around me for people I might recruit on a mission to run down into the ring and save the bull's life.

A young mother is teaching her toddler to hurl peanuts down at the ring.

"Repita," she tells him. "Vaya a tu casa, pendejo!"

"Vaya a tu casa, pendejo," yells the boy at the matador, chucking another nut.

"Que buéno," says the mother. "Otra vez."

The bullfighter has already saluted the judge, but I can see the bull is still panting in a puddle of blood. Out jogs a paunchy Pink-Socks in a torero suit he bought before acquiring his gut. This old-timer hasn't been in the ring yet; he was lurking behind the wall during the fight, and now I see the flash of a dagger so slight he can conceal it in one hand. He tiptoes up behind the bull's head and looking around I see no one is even watching and then without meaning to, I yell:

"Somebody stop that man!" My eyes and throat are burning. "He has a knife!"

There is an instant of silence around me, and then a burst of laughter.

"Mira el gringo! Llorando, llorando."

"Pobrecito yanqui. Le gusta el torito."

I don't know what they're saying; maybe I've recruited

some helpers. I look around at the jeering faces. And then the Pink-Socks with the dagger, bending over as matter-of-factly as if he had dropped his car keys, rams the little knife straight into the bull's brain, probing in tight circles like he's scraping the meat from a coconut. The animal kicks its feet and lurches in a final spasm and only now do we realize that positively it's dead. The assassin wipes his nasty little switchblade clean on the bull's hide and creeps back to his hiding place.

I should have done something. What kind of coward was I to let that happen? I'm an American: We don't let this sort of torture go unpunished. Out comes a squad of guys dressed like milkmen who rake the puddles of blood. With chains and a wooden yoke they harness a pair of draft horses to the carcass, moving with frightening expertise. The dead bull gets a final round of boos as he's hauled out through the tunnel.

And with one bull dead, there are five more to go. Nobody kills on the first try, and throughout the afternoon the bloody swords bounce in the dirt. One bull is especially strong, and the crowd chants *toro toro* and the bull refuses to die, jumping up at the bearer of the switchblade as if to yell, Fuck you, I'm not dead yet. And once it's finally dead and the pizzas are selling, the judge signals the milkmen to trot the carcass in a victory lap, and people stand and applaud, which Travis LaFrance realizes is a fine tradition, a noble and respectful salute to the animal, or at least to its eternal soul, like you might do for a war hero, but on the other hand, shit, people, who are you trying to kid? YOU KILLED HIM! And it's debatable whether or not his eternal soul gives a shit that his mortal carcass, limp and bloody and strapped to a horse, gets a standing ovation from a bunch of perfectly alive assholes gulping cerveza and gobbling hot dogs.

With each killing I have a vision that I know is wrong to have, but it keeps coming back: I picture myself running down the stands and leaping into the ring and flinging myself over the bull and crying, "Stop this madness! Let this creature live! This should not be allowed!" But I don't do anything except sit there alone and open my notebook.

"Today's corrida was a thing of beauty," I write. "How brave the man, how noble the beast, how profound the ritual! My eyes are still wet with the tears I've wept: tears borne from the sheer glory and art of the ceremony I've seen."

CHAPTER SEVEN

MEXICO CITY OFFERED MORE TO AN EXILE than I had originally thought. I abandoned the plan of roughing it through dusty ranchos and instead rented an apartment in a nice part of town. I was finding that actual travel upset my stomach and stifled my creativity, and that I wrote better if I stayed put. And since the dollar sign and the peso sign are the same, I could pretend I was rich. The bank machine seemed to tell me I had ten thousand dollars. I bought dinner with a hundred-spot and paid the cab fare with a fifty. Forget all that dust and sweat and hardship: Más sushi, amigo, and keep the change.

Mexico City belonged to Travis LaFrance. At the sight of me strolling past my doorman, those grimy buildings on Avenida Coyoacan shook off the soot and sat up straight to become the crisp tableau for the major prose stylist in their midst. Jacaranda trees lining the avenue launched flowers into the sky that exploded purple overhead and wafted to the ground like confetti at a banquet in my honor. Guards with flak jackets and shotguns came to attention in the doorways of banks, and cops collecting pesos from people parked in the red shot an admiring glance from behind mirrored sunglasses. Claro, Señor LaFrance, they seemed to tell me. Por

Claro, Señor LaFrance. Por supuesto. Mexico City law enforcers appreciate an expatriate artist in their midst.

supuesto. The Volkswagen taxis came bouncing down the avenue like runaway limes spilled from the barrel of a fruit vendor who knew I needed a ride. But I waved the cabbies on: Muchas gracias, but I'll walk on my own two feet. Amid the honking horns and squealing tires was the sizzle of my lunch frying in the taco carts and the whir of blenders stuffed with mango and the sad plaint of the accordion's ballad. Its owner jingled a change cup and I tossed him a heavy coin.

As an expatriate should, I found a café where I could write. Café CyberMundo was so serious a haven for writers that instead of coffee or absinthe or crossaints, it provided only computers. For twenty pesos an hour I could join a writers' community where a dozen fellow artists sat in front of flickering screens, no doubt toiling at their sonnets, short stories, and heroic couplets. CyberMundo inspired its writers by blasting synthesized dance pop, though sometimes the music so overstimulated me that I couldn't even express myself in words, and in secret I began tucking foam plugs into my ears to tone down the muse a bit. Once I brought a bottle of beer to my computer to accentuate my bohemian tendencies, but the manager told me it wasn't allowed, and I had to pour it down the toilet.

My one disappointment with CyberMundo was that it allowed access to the Internet. I had assumed that e-mail hadn't yet reached Mexico, and that instead I'd get to communicate with my editor through telegram, something to the tune of:

MUCH BLOOD IN THE SAND STOP WIRE ME 5000 PESOS TO HOTEL MONTE CARLO IN MEXICO CITY CARE OF LA SENORITA LADY VICTORIA DE LA CARTEGENA PASCAL DE SEVILLA STOP ABRAZOS TRAVIS STOP

But I turned the technology to my advantage: The Internet made me a better writer. Instead of simply staring dumbly at the blank page as have less fortunate generations of writers, I was able to gain instant access to information on an infinite variety of topics. I found bullfight programs from Peru dating back to 1999, I read weather reports from Madrid and Granada, and I joined a number of e-based taurine clubs, sending queries to their members, introducing myself, and seeking advice on how to proceed with my project.

Unfortunately, the Mexican technology was still somewhat lacking, and due to some faulty connection most of my e-mails went unanswered. But overall the Internet allowed me to spend much more time at the computer than previously imagined, and to do more work, assuming that we measure productivity in terms of information viewed and data consumed instead of using some antiquated yardstick such as number of pages written.

One morning an e-mail came from the editor in New York.

Travis: The publisher and I will be in Madrid in May to see a few corridas. What dates will you be there? Let's plan to meet up. How is the book coming? —Ed.

BULLFIGHTING EXCELLENT HERE IN MEXICO STOP FINDING NEW WORLD PERMUTATIONS OF OLD WORLD TRADITION PERHAPS BEST FOCUS FOR TORO STOP TRAVEL TO SPAIN PERHAPS SUPERFLUOUS AT THIS POINT STOP ABRAZOS TRAVIS

Travis: I pray that I misunderstood your note. Surely you are not considering not going to Spain. If so, this is a serious concern, and we need to talk directly. Please call me collect right away. —Ed.

YOUR LAST TRANSMISSION GARBLED STOP POWER OUTAGE HERE IN MEXICO STOP PLEASE RESEND YOUR MESSAGE NEXT WEEK STOP ABRAZOS TRAVIS

Like Hemingway's Jake Barnes battling the Republicans in Spain, Travis quickly got his chance to set down the pen and take up the sword. For a decade rebels in the state of Chiapas had been firing guns and making demands and getting on television, standing up for the indigenous people kept down by the government. Their spokesman Subcomandante Marcos rode a horse and waved a machine gun as he denounced racism and imperialism from behind his black ski mask. Just as I arrived in Mexico City the Zapatistas left the safety of their jungle camps for the first time and marched on the capital.

Fate must have smiled, to have placed Travis and Marcos in the same city on the same day. The Zapatista National Liberation Army left Chiapas with a caravan of police motorcycles and press vans and a slick tour bus called the Marcosmobile that, according to my dictionary, read Heading for the Sun on the bulletproof windshield. Behind it, Marcos smoked his pipe and waved at compañeros. Along the way they were joined by activists from France and Italy and, yes, by Travis himself.

Recall the chapter in *Toro* when LaFrance hops the barricade and joins arms with the rebels as they march toward the Zócalo. He is wearing his ski mask and speaking fluent Spanish, so it's not until they reach the rally with half a million ecstatic marchers that Travis reveals himself to be a white American. The rebels are mildly surprised but by then have learned that what's on the inside is more important than skin color, and they welcome him as one of their own.

"Amigo," says Comandante Felipe, "we march as friends."

"No, hermano," says Travis LaFrance, "we march as brothers."

As always, I used my fictional license to portray Travis in the noble light he demands. This is not to say that my own interactions with the Zapatistas lacked valor. My notes from that Sunday give a step-by-step account of my meeting:

1. I get off the metro at Piño Suarez, not sure where the Zócalo is, but see a mass of people moving up the street, so I follow them. Along the way all sorts of things are for sale, mostly black T-shirts with pictures of Marcos, revolutionary slogans, and, on the back, dates and towns of the Zapa-

tour, just like a rock concert jersey. But the first product I buy is this little spiral device for cutting carrots and zucchinis into interesting spring-like shapes: vegetable slinkys, you could call them. A fast-talking dude is giving a dazzling demonstration of what he can do to potatoes, even apples, a live version of a late-night infomercial. I can't understand him, but who cares. At fifteen pesos, people are buying like crazy. The man takes my money and gives me change without missing a beat in his spiel, arranging a cucumber in an elegant coil, whapping the device against his hand to show how safe it is.

2. The crowd thickens at the Zócalo. Longhaired students pass out pamphlets and newspapers. I buy a copy of *La Machete*, the revolutionary newspaper of workers and farmers, from a girl with pink hair, a nose ring, and a jcrew.com baseball hat. For sale are pins and shirts with not only Marcos but also Che Guevara, Emiliano Zapata, Pancho Villa, the hammer and sickle, and the pop singer Manu Chau, who's not actually a rebel leader but, like Travis LaFrance, lends artistic credibility to the cause. Also selling briskly are black ski masks, a real show of commitment, considering it's approaching eighty degrees of bright sunshine. Briefly I consider purchasing a key chain modeled after Marcos's trademark tobacco pipe but am whisked away by the crowd, and figure there will be better stuff to come.

3. Get close enough to a big stage to see a woman singing folk songs of the revolution. Wander. First sighting of Incredibly Beautiful Exotic Woman #1. Decide to follow her, seek chance for casual introduction. She is taking photos. I wonder if she is a student and begin thinking up suitable opening lines: Why are you taking pictures? is the best I can conjure with my limited Spanish. Just as I have IBEW#1

in my range—she's pricing ski masks, for real—I am railroaded by a young woman claiming to write for a Spanish newspaper who wants my opinion of the goings-on. I'm sort of flattered that someone is asking me questions in Spanish, so I answer as best I can, telling her that it's pretty exciting to see hammers and sickles and people chanting for revolution, because we don't get that in the States, but to be honest I don't exactly understand what Marcos and the Zapatistas are asking for, and can't really say whether or not they should get it. I proceed to tell her I am in Mexico to write a book about bullfighting, not because she has asked or because she cares, but because it's a series of sentences I have rehearsed that makes me seem pretty fluent. She dutifully takes my name and age, and copies my quotes, and by the time she leaves, IBEW#1 has escaped, and after a few futile laps to find her, I move on.

4. Here I find the heart of the Marcos memorabilia marketplace. Purchase a color photo of the Subcomandante smoking his pipe (ten pesos) and a mounted Pancho Villa poster (twenty pesos), inviting gringos to join him in overthrowing the Mexican government. I see a really cool pyramid-shaped Marcos paperweight, but the asking price of twenty-five pesos seems a bit steep, and I'm not sure about the manners for bargaining with vendors of leftist propaganda. I mean: If it were huaraches or serapes the lady were selling, I'd offer half, then bid back and forth, but this isn't really a tourist item, and mightn't it be a grievous insult for a gringo to try to save, like, seventy-five cents on a Marcos paperweight, proceeds from which will undoubtedly finance the overthrow of the capitalist regime and quicken the dawn of a classless society? So I keep walking, my fingers twitching for that paperweight. Anyway, I tell myself,

I'm holding out for a Subcomandante Marcos action figure. It's getting hotter. Buy a five-peso lime-flavored ice concoction to support the cause.

5. Walk past a group performing traditional Aztec dance, with plumed headdresses and incense and drums, then finally find the action figure I covet. The woman explains that some have adjustable arms, others not. Buy the one with movable limbs (thirty pesos) so I can make him salute. Some man follows me and asks me questions about my interest in the event, apparently incredulous at the sight of a grown-up gringo buying a Subcomandante Marcos action figure with movable arms. Give the speech about the bullfighting book, which seems to satisfy him.

6. Press up against barricade to watch the arrival of the Marcosmobile, preceded by a flatbed tractor trailer upon which a dozen or more Zapatistas in ski masks are waving to the madly cheering crowd, the whole procession ringed by locked-arm supporters, chanting, "E-Z-L-N. E-Z-L-N." Someone has gone limp and is carried away. Heat stroke? Trampling? Who knows? Once the trailer is empty, I wait for the door of the Marcosmobile to open, to get my first glimpse of this historical person, a momentous occasion, akin to seeing Martin Luther King march on Washington or Fidel Castro arrive in Havana (assuming he arrived in Havana; I don't actually know my Cuban history, but he must have). I want to be a part of it, to witness history, to feel the pulse of the masses, of the movement, of the Great March. But the bus door does not open. The crowd roars as the Zapatistas line up on the stage. Then it hits me: I missed it. Marcos was on the trailer, and he is already gone. History paraded right before my eyes and I didn't see it.

7. Relocate to a new spot to view the Subcomandante. But from where I stand, they all look the same: a bunch of dudes in fatigues and ski masks. What's worse, some guy up front is blocking my view with this huge fucking indigenous plumed headdress, like an entire peacock in heat perched on his head. People atop shoulders, taking photos, crowd tightening, yelling "Down in front," me having flashbacks to near-death trampling experience at high school rock concert. I retreat.

8. Am drawn back toward vicinity of Marcos pyramid-shaped paperweight, but suddenly catch glimpse of Incredibly Beautiful Exotic Woman #2. My chest seizes. Look at her marvelous brown shoulders, that black hair, and those black eyes: the embodiment of the native beauty that has inspired this gathering. And even better, she's dressed kind of hip: an Aztec princess in flared Levis. As Travis's consort she'll personify modern Mexico, with her roots in the jungle temples but her sneakers on the city pavement.

I follow her and begin rehearsing opening lines:

"Te gusta el subcomandante tambien?" or maybe "Revolución es como amor, no?"

I lose her. I wander five minutes, maybe ten, find her again, ducked under a vendor's umbrella, and I tone down my speech for simplicity: Hace mucho calor, I will say, and I haven't really figured out what I'll say next—it's now or never—but just as I approach, a gust of wind knocks over the umbrella and she scurries off, and the moment is lost. I begin surveillance, ascertaining that she is alone and looking for someone, craning her neck, standing tippy-toed. Perhaps she traveled here from her village with her father, and now she can't find him. By now I've looked at her at least twenty times, but we've never made eye contact, and I'm sure she sees me and knows what I'm up to and is trying to ditch me as hard as I'm trying to catch her. She smokes a cigarette—what a perfect anachronism for this Mayan goddess!—and just as I am about to bum one from her, some other asshole beats me to it, and from a distance I can tell she doesn't have one, either she bummed the one she had or it was her last. Suddenly I lose her again. I begin desperate laps. *Toro* needs this woman. Travis needs this woman. He can't join the insurgency without a brown-skinned love interest. Over the loudspeakers, voices thunder on about dignity and peace and justice, echoing back and forth between the majestic palace and church. Also something about people of color and Yankee imperialism, but I can't totally understand it, and besides I'm focused on finding my black-eyed princess. I needn't be too concerned with what they're saying: My art should transcend politics. Anyway, they don't seem to need another foot soldier for the cause. Probably the best way for an American of no color to show his solidarity, I think, is to publicly stand aloof from the name-calling while privately breaking down racial barriers by getting to know this really hot girl of color, and then writing a novella about it. I decide to find the guy selling the pipe key chains, which can't be more than five pesos, but am rebuffed by the thick crowd, so it's back to the marketplace, where there aren't many people because you can't see the stage at all, unless you've purchased these clever periscopes fashioned from candy boxes and mirrors for sale for ten pesos, and just then when I'm totally demoralized . . .

9. There she is, IBEW#2, as stunning and as lost as ever, and I practically lunge at her.

"Hace mucho calor," I say perfectly.

"Sí, mucho."

"Te gusta el subcomandante?"

"Mucho."

It's going even better than I'd hoped.

"De donde eres?" I say.

"Vienna."

"En que estado es?"

"Austria."

"Es cerca de aquí?"

"No. Austria is in Europe."

I ignore the language lapse and continue in Spanish. English is so pedestrian. She tells me she's been separated from her two amigas and doesn't think she'll find them. Yes, I say, there are a lot of people here. She agrees, and we continue to chat. Those black Aztec eyes turn out to be blue, and those wonderful brown shoulders are not the indigenous color of soil but the result of five months bumming on the beaches of Mexico. But contrasted against the faded orange of her stylish tank top, they're no less pretty.

As she answers my questions she keeps peeking over my shoulder, and I ask her if she's hungry and wants to get something to eat, but no, she's thirsty, so we find a lady selling drinks and we each get a bottle of water, and I say let me, handing over the money for both, always the gentleman, and then I tell her the bit about the bullfighting book, because it's four o'clock and I ought be heading over to the plaza de toros and by now I'll settle for a European companion on my arm.

"Do you like the killing?" she says.

I nod stoically. "Es un arte."

My Austrian scrunches up her face and says she loves

animals, she could never watch them get killed, and I feel like a brute, a jerk, and assure her that this march, this rally, whatever you call it, is much more important than a bullfight.

She announces she's leaving. I can't tell where she's going, but I'm pretty sure I'm not invited. "Maybe I'll see you around," she says and shrugs and smiles and shakes my hand, and there's this awkward moment where I realize IBEW#2 is about to leave me, and I'm not quick-witted enough to invite myself along or ask for a phone number, and then she gives me a peck on the cheek and is lost in the masses.

I stand there dumbfounded. I sit down on the curb, sure she'll be right back, and this time I'll be ready, make plans, set something up, but she doesn't come back, and what can I do but head across town to the stupid brutish cruel bullfight, where you'll never in a million years run across some Austrian hippie girl with shoulders freshly tanned from the Mexican beaches, and I tell myself that I've done something good and pure, you know, buying the water for her, she didn't seem to have any money on her, but good intentions do nothing to get those fine shoulders off my mind, and trudging down Avenida de la Católica, gulping from my newly bought bottle of water, the streets that had for a moment blossomed in blue and orange and sunshine and promise are once again gray and dirty and foreign, a city of thirty million people I'll never know.

CHAPTER EIGHT

———

TORO'S MOST SUBLIME MOMENT COMES WHEN Carmen, the teenage torera, gives Travis the ear of the bull she's just killed.

"Travisito," she whispers, wiping the blood from her brow. Her hair is pulled back beneath a derby hat. Her breast heaves beneath the suspenders of her traje corto. She stands in a heap of roses in the empty bullring. "You have known many women, and I am just a girl."

"Quiet, my little rabbit," says Travis LaFrance.

"Soon you will return to your homeland in el norte, and you will forget about the little girl named Carmen who fights bulls."

"I shall not forget thee, rabbit."

"Take me back with you, Travisito! I will be good and do all that you instruct me."

Why not marry her? Mr. and Mrs. Travis LaFrance of Moab, Utah. It's pretty to think about it now, but that which we do is never as pretty as that which we think about. It's all nada, anyhow. Nada y nada y pues nada.

"Kiss me, child," says Travis LaFrance.

"With you, Travisito, I felt the earth fall away beneath me."

"I felt it, too, little rabbit."

"Then take this," she moans. She presses the bull's ear into his palm. "Today it is warm and filled with blood, like my heart. Take it to your cabin in the desert and mount it on the mantel with your other trophies. And when it turns hard and dry remember the heart of little Carmen."

"Thy heart is young, Carmen. It shall not harden."

Travis kisses away the tears from her cheek.

"Perhaps you are right and I am just a foolish girl. But the hurt inside me is of an old woman."

"The hurt is inside me also, child. The hurt is always with me."

Travis LaFrance pulls Carmen close. She cries.

"Don't make me say another word, Travisito. Every word is a hurt. Hold me until it's time to go."

I first found her in Viveros de Coyoacan. Cortez must have been thinking of me when he planted this nursery, because there among the groves of eucalyptus and palm and walnut was a pleasantly shaded oval where I could watch the bull-fighters practice. The toreros worked in pairs, one with a cape and the other with bull horns. They danced together in slow motion, the bull grunting and inching the horns toward the cape while the other arched like a ballerina. Old men in derby hats and windbreakers sat on the bench all day, now getting up to make a few passes with the cape, then cracking pistachios with their teeth and spitting the shells. Someone jogged out to the street to fetch a few Cokes to pass around. Nothing else mattered. No one had a job or any concerns besides the cape and the sword. This was the essential.

And then I saw Carmen. A girl bullfighter! Waving the cape in her warm-up suit and sneakers, Carmen looked as much like a tennis player as a torera. I'd have her wear something more exotic for the book. I moved to a bench where I could watch her better, and in an instant she blossomed, like Proust's cookie, into the passionate, sensual, and tortured damsel you remember from *Toro*. My Carmen is uncorrupted by modernity, pulsing with blood more pure and rich than those anemic American girls bottle-fed with computers and career counseling. She picked up the sword. I watched how her delicate fingers gripped the handle and my imagination convulsed. Disempowered by Mexican patriarchy, Carmen is drawn to the sword for the phalloerotic strength it embodies. Killing bulls releases not only her feminist rage, but also her untapped sexual fury, and each thrust of the sword whips her into a primal frenzy. But she had to be gentle, too, so as she snapped the sword before me, I decided that in the arms of Travis LaFrance her bloodlust would wash away and she'd be tender as a kitten.

Her cell phone rang.

It was sitting on the bench beside me. I'd noticed it there but hadn't imagined that it belonged to Carmen. We both looked at it. Carmen tried to concentrate on her veronicas but the phone kept ringing.

"Contéstalo, por favor."

I clicked the button and said, "Bueno." A boy wanted to talk to her.

"Ella está toreando," I said. Carmen put down the cape and answered the call. The guy calling was a classmate, and she told him to meet her at four o'clock and they'd study together. When she hung up I asked if she was studying poems of the fiesta brava, but instead she had a chemistry test the next day. My bullfighter was a senior in high school.

Carmen had showed me a poster advertising a corrida she was in, and invited me to come. When the day came I couldn't find a companion, so I decided to go it alone and asked directions from the old toreros eating pistachios on the park benches. It's very difficult, said one. You won't be able to find it. You'll be fine, said another. All you need to do is take a metro to Estación del Norte and a bus to Aculco and then a pesero out to Bañe. None recalled the numbers of the routes, but they had a vague idea where I'd find them.

I reached Estación del Norte without incident, then boarded an economy-class bus that inched out of Mexico City in freeway gridlock. The woman at the ticket counter had not heard of Bañe, but directed me to a bus that stopped in Aculco. I told the fat man sitting next to me where I was going and he'd never heard of it. As a last resort I consulted my guidebook. Neither Bañe nor Aculco were listed in the index.

Then I noticed Carmen in the front of the bus. She must have boarded after me. I wondered if she would remember me. She definitely didn't know my name. I decided to play it cool and not say anything; instead, I would follow her. The bus rumbled up the highway for two hours, then turned off onto a country road for a while before slowing for the speed bumps at some dusty village of white plaster. Carmen stepped off the bus and I hoisted my bag and followed. When I hit the sidewalk she was already gone. I scanned the plaza and saw her ducking into a taxi. When I ran over she was in the backseat with a man.

"Van a la corrida?"

"Sí."

"Puedo venir?"

"Sí."

I climbed in the taxi and we bumped over the cobblestone. Carmen's companion wore jeans and a plaid shirt. He didn't look like much competition for Travis LaFrance. They spoke Spanish, and, remarkably, I could translate what they were saying.

"Where is your sword, love?" he said.

"Ay, matador! I left it on the bus."

"Driver, follow that bus."

We bounced down the road and the taxi passed the bus and stopped in front. Carmen jumped out and retrieved her sword from the luggage compartment. Her companion shook his head in disappointment, and once we were moving again I introduced myself and asked if he was a novillero, too.

He laughed. "She is a novice. I am a killer."

I hadn't recognized him without his pink socks. He was the matador Alfredo Lopez, who'd fought in the Plaza Mexico on Sunday. He didn't know where we were going either. We turned off the blacktop onto a dirt road without signs, just a piece of cardboard that said TOROS, past bony cows huddling in the shade of shrubs, across the hilly countryside to a dusty village with a pink church. I took advantage of having him as a chaperone and asked her some questions. I wanted to know firsthand the blinding passion that propelled her toward fame. I asked if she had many fans who came to watch her.

"Sometimes my parents, but today they're at work."

I asked what her plans were after high school.

"I'd like to study business." She said she'd probably give up bullfighting next year when she went to college.

But didn't she want to become a full-fledged matadora? I asked. There was only one in Mexico and she could be the second.

"It would take a lot of work. Someday I'd like to go to the United States and work in advertising or television. I have some cousins in Texas."

Carmen told me she had been fighting bulls for three years, and so far she had killed one bull. Just to hear her say the word kill made my lungs tighten.

"Did you love it?" I asked breathlessly. "How did it make you feel?"

"It was okay. Alfredo, let's stop for a Coke."

He had the driver pull off at a roadside tienda. As we filed out of the car I realized breathlessly that I'd just held an entire conversation in Spanish and understood everything.

Part of what makes Toro such a poetic success, and puts it in the ranks of other classic bullfighting books, is the way I was able to capture the archaic formality of the Spanish language. I learned from Hemingway that if you translate the words directly, even the most mundane conversations seem profound. As evidenced by this excerpt, I even improved on Hemingway's style by including Spanish punctuation:

"¿What shall we buy, my love?" said Alfredo.

"Tostitos, killer, and two cans of Coke."

"¿Do you want a refreshment?" the killer asked me.

"I do not have thirst."

"It is very distant to the bullfight. Perhaps you are going to have thirst."

"You have reason. I will have thirst."

"Come and see the refreshments," said the female novice.

Inside the refrigerator we saw the juice of the brand Boing.

"Missus," said the killer. "¿In what flavors are the Boing?"

"Mango and guava, young man."

The killer looked at me and I said, "Mango."

"A refreshment of guava for myself and one of mango for the fair-skinned."

The woman opened the refrigerator.

"I'm sorry, guero. We lack mango. Only guava."

"Fine, then. Two of guava."

"¿In bottles or little bags, young man?"

"In little bags, please. We will take them in the coach."

She set the plastic bags of the guava-flavored Boing refreshment on the counter while the killer laid flat two coins of ten pesos, and I wrapped my fingers around the bottle. I felt the icy droplets on my palm. It was as cold as any bottle I had ever held.

"Agitate it," said the killer, and I shook. The particles of guava floated upward and swirled pink and cold in the fruit-looking bottle. The killer opened a plastic sandwich bag and I emptied the liquid into the bag and the killer took the red drinking-straw from the hand of the storekeeper and placed it in the bag of juice and tied the corners in a square knot.

"Good," said the killer. "We go.

"¿Does the Boing please you, guero?"

"The Boing pleases me well, killer."

I'd come a long way since my first bullfight. Now I was arriving in the same car as the toreros. A true aficionado. I anticipated our taxi getting bogged down in a gauntlet of paparazzi and the Spanish trumpets playing a stirring ballad as we were ushered to the luxury boxes. Carmen would emerge in her suit of lights and red lips and slay the massive monster with her slender sword.

But the only person we had to dodge was a drunk asleep in the street. The town bullring was an erector set of rickety benches that would probably be taken down by carnies in the morning. I followed Alfredo underneath the bleachers, where we would have the best view. A quartet of electric guitars, drums, and accordion skittered out a fast ranchera *oom-pah-pah*.

There were no horses at this bullfight. With the flatbed backed up to the ring, a cowboy stood on top and lanced the bull, then they pulled the chute and it rushed out. The bull was little and knock-kneed and tripped on its goofy feet. Carmen appeared in slacks and suspenders, with her hair braided beneath a man's hat. She looked like a shepherd. The little bull knocked her over and she rolled in the dirt shielding her head. When she got up and patted the dust off her knees, the announcer called for applause and the drunk men wearing cowboy hats gave a cheer. The village schoolgirls were clustered in the front row in uniforms licking lollipops and chanting *torera torera*.

And then something shook me: The first bullfighter could not kill his bull. After nine stabs someone else ran out to help, but the problem was that the helper was wearing jeans and a wristwatch. As he waved the muleta, coins spilled from his pocket and he bent over to pick them up. Without the costume he was not a matador, just a guy with a weapon. It wasn't right. They finally lured the bull toward a mean little man hiding beneath the bleachers in slacks and cowboy boots and a western shirt. The man reached from behind the barrera and sunk his switchblade into the bull's brain. The dagger-man hopped the fence and slit its throat. Some people booed and others clapped.

"This is not real bullfighting," Alfredo Lopez told me.

There were no horses to haul out the dead bull. Three vaqueros looped a yellow rope over the head and lined up like a tug-of-war team. The bull didn't budge. Someone's hand was dripping with blood, having just been fiddling with the jugular vein, and he stared at it like a wound, wondering where to wipe. They tried dragging again, this time from the tail, but still the bull wouldn't move. In puttered a dented pickup, and, lighting cigarettes, the men heaved the carcass into the bed and drove off.

If the first kill were any indication, these amateurs might not be good enough to appear in my book. I hoped my heroine wouldn't embarrass me.

But Carmen fought her bull well. When it was time to kill, Alfredo gestured to the band to cut the music, but they played on anyway. Carmen poised herself with the sword. Her first stab went deep, but the bull didn't die. She pulled out the sword and stabbed again. The bull fell. Everyone cheered and Alfredo Lopez cut an ear and presented it to her.

When it was over, Carmen circled the ring with the capote outstretched like a bedsheet to catch coins tossed from the seats. The money landed in the dirt and she dug for it with bare fingers. She signed autographs for the little girls. The teenage boys whistled catcalls and skimmed their cowboy hats at her feet, then jumped bareback on skinny horses and trotted off sucking liter bottles of beer.

Carmen had performed admirably, and I decided to keep her in my book after all. Besides, darkness was falling, and I had no idea how I was going to get back to Mexico City. I chased down Carmen and Alfredo to beg a ride home—consider the irony of asking favors from characters in your own book!—and they invited me to dinner at the ranch down the road.

I looked at the car: a late-model Plymouth K car that belonged to another torero's girlfriend's father. Typically I travel with a bit more class, but I said that would be fine. I was a bit disappointed when Alfredo Lopez had to put on glasses in order to drive, and when offered a beer he said he didn't drink. I expected a matador to be a bit more robust.

At the ranch, two dozen fellow aficionados and toreros lined the banquet tables on the veranda in the shade of big trees. I tried to get a seat next to Carmen, but both were taken, so I sat with the ranch hands. "We who love toros are a family," said the vaquero sitting next to me. "Welcome." He poured me a plastic cup of tequila. Jugs of soda and styrofoam bowls appeared, followed by gruel with fat bubbles floating on top, then pork, lots of it, fresh out of the fire, with beans and rice and tortillas and salsa. A bare lightbulb dangled from a wire overhead. A roll of toilet paper was passed around. The girls in aprons refilled the bowls of cilantro and green salsa. I diluted my liquor with soda pop and raised it for one toast after another. I still couldn't get in a word with Carmen. After dinner, I sneaked outside to look for an outhouse.

There I met the man upon whom I based Don Carlos, the mystical seer whose brief appearance in *Toro* is sure to incite controversy among literary critics. Don Carlos mentors Travis on the mythic importance of the bullfight and the pure soul of the Mexican people, thus providing the intellectual foundations for the truths that our narrator had intuitively understood. Then, in a flourish of drama and mystery, Don Carlos, the Mexican wise man, morphs into a raven and soars into the horizon.

What follows here is the actual conversation upon which I based that scene. Frankly, I felt some of what he said was difficult and confusing, so in the book I altered it to a more clear defense of bullfighting.

"Call me Don Carlos, guero," the man said as I exited the outhouse. He flattened his windblown hair with his hand. "Tell me what you think of my country, and my people."

"I like it very much."

"You are norteamericano, no?"

"Sí."

"What do your paisanos think of Mexico?"

"They imagine a man with a mustache and a sombrero and pistols on his belt." We were speaking a bit higher-level Spanish than I was used to.

"Pancho Villa," he said.

"Sí. Pancho Villa."

"What do you write about, guero?"

"Bullfighting."

"These are the things of stereotypes," he said, waving a hand at the feast. "Bullfighting is as foreign to me as it is to you. You will find that this country is much more varied than your paisanos believe, and that at the end of the story, we Mexicans are just the same as Americans, the same as people everywhere. We are thinkers."

"Do you like la fiesta brava?" I said.

"I don't feel any real emotion at a bullfight," said Don Carlos. "There is no drama because the outcome is certain. I prefer basketball. Or football."

"But what about the tradition?"

"It is not a Mexican tradition. It's Spanish. And the bullfight is just a spectacle for the public. Without the public there would be no bullfight. It is an egotistical art."

Just then the party was breaking up and Carmen approached the outhouse. Don Carlos stopped her.

"Tell me, torera: Would the bullfight exist without an audience?"

She didn't know she had walked into his trap. I hoped she would defy him and prove that bullfighting was profound.

"Is the toilet available?" she said.

"Would you kill the bull if nobody watched?"

"I don't think so. No, of course not."

"Gracias, torera." He let her go on her way, and the door slammed shut behind her. He turned to me. "You see: It is a commercial art and an egotistical art, not an authentic art."

"Then what is authentic?"

"Do you believe in reincarnation, or in resurrection?"

"No hay pinche papeles," said Carmen from the outhouse.

Mysteriously, Don Carlos produced a strip of toilet paper from his pocket. He folded it neatly and slid it under the door.

"Let's go," I said. "Give a girl some privacy." Don Carlos asked if I believe in creation or evolution. I tried to answer as Travis LaFrance would.

"I think that after we die we turn into dust."

"That can't be," he said. "Where does imagination come from? Without our minds we are less than animals. Animals at least have instinct. Without imagination we are robots. We are without conscience. This is why I don't like the bullfights. The matador is without conscience."

"Does that mean he is not authentic?"

"Do you understand the Bible?"

"Some of it."

"Is it authentic or commercial?"

"Authentic."

"Until you understand the Bible, you cannot be a writer. You cannot be an apostle of the truth."

It was time to go. Carmen had exited the outhouse and was loading into the K car, and I was afraid they'd leave without me. "So if you write for the reader your work is not authentic?"

"You must write for yourself. It must be personal, not commercial. The writer must have no ego. His work is a service to mankind."

"Like Tolstoy," I said. *"Crime and Punishment."*

"Yes," he said with a puzzled look. "Tolstoy. At the end of the story, we are all the same. We all eat bread. It comes in different forms, but it is the same everywhere."

I wished he would turn into a raven and fly off so I wouldn't miss my ride. We shook hands and I ran to the car.

I wanted to see the ear. I knew from my reading that the ear had mythical importance. Bullfighters gave them to lovers and mentors and parents and statesmen. I stood behind the car, and as Carmen was zipping her bag I asked to see the ear. She wasn't sure where it was, but after asking inside the car, she located it and dropped it in my palm. It was soft and pliable. She watched me finger it.

"Do you want it?" she said.

For a moment I doubted myself. The ear was a sacred trophy from the second bull she'd ever killed; she should give it to her lover or el presidente. Was I really worthy of such a gift?

"Don't you want it?" I said.

"It's yours," she said with a shrug. "It doesn't matter to me."

Of course I was worthy. I was Travis LaFrance. The ear was warm in my hand. Carmen's eyes in the fading sunlight turned the color of honey.

"I will not forget thee, Carmen. I will hold it close to my heart."

"Put it in a plastic bag. And cover it with salt."

"Thank you, my lady."

"You don't want it to rot."

I reached for her hand to kiss it, but instead she shook mine, then let go. I held the dead ear. The matador rapped on the roof of the K car and told us to hurry. I gazed into the eyes of fair Carmenita. She slammed the trunk and ushered me to the back door.

"We are five in this car," she said. "You must sit in the middle."

CHAPTER NINE

———

READERS WILL WANT TO KNOW HOW MUCH of Travis LaFrance is me and how much is made up. They're right in doubting that a hero so rich, memorable, and real could have simply sprung from my mind. I didn't just invent Travis. He emerged half-formed in San Francisco in the spring of my twenty-second year, and came to life some months later, fertilized by a dancer I'd met.

I graduated from public school believing that my birthright as an American was to succeed at whatever I pursued. Like Mark Twain and Jack London and Ernest Hemingway, I wanted to write adventure books for the Common Man, and at age seventeen I determined that a fancy university would prepare me for this work. Experts at the college would teach me at once to spin a good yarn and speak for the masses.

But instead the experts branded me with the same scarlet P that they stamped on those wards of the trust fund and the prep school. Turned out I was not the Common Man, but the Privileged Son. The pronouncement didn't sit quite right, considering we didn't even have color TV at home, but was irrefutable. Even if I didn't have money and family connections, I was told, I had opportunities: I came from a safe white suburb with good free schools. Forget about the sweat and blood and justice, they said; a member of your class can never understand that. Instead, sign on the line and we'll set you up in advertising or consulting and give you the combination to the country club gate and—what's that? You say you want to be a writer? You want hardship? Well, there's plenty of suffering to write about in *our own class*: self-hatred, white guilt, squandered fortunes, and valium addiction, for starters, and if you want real drama, write about your materialistic and dysfunctional family and how it's their fault you ended up working for Arthur Andersen.

I had stumbled into a private society that winked and understood that books were written simply to give professors a lesson plan, and professors were hired simply to stimulate the prince's intellect as he prepared for a dalliance on Wall Street. I tried my hardest to fit in. If spiritual hardship required driving a luxury car and living in a gated neighborhood, then I guessed I could aspire to it. I dissected my childhood, combing the soccer fields and camping trips for evidence of privilege, condemning myself and my parents for our contentment, embellishing the most tepid disagreements to find the pain that would prove my theorem: *If* I am a writer, and *if* all writers suffer, *then* I must have suffered at some point. It was just a matter of remembering.

But the stories I wrote sucked, and it was all my parents' fault. How did they expect me to peal away my class's facade of propriety and reveal its ugly corrupt soul when instead of being alcoholic and deluded, they were sort of nice, and modest, and loving? They weren't even divorced. In a fit of indignation I saw that my parents had deprived me of the suffering I needed to be a serious artist, and that I would never write a convincing tragedy of privilege.

With embarrassment and regret I turned my back on my class. Forget about the stock portfolios and the yacht and the therapist—I would settle for my own B-grade version of the American Dream: tasting the soil and breathing the stars and writing my books. Relinquish, I whispered to myself, relinquish. But as I prepared to donate my bourgeois loot to the underclass, I realized I didn't have anything to give away.

Fine: There was still the American ghetto. Further reneging on my class obligations, I flung myself into the gut of San Francisco, intent on besmirching my innocence and dismantling my privilege. Rent was cheap in the Western Addition, just blocks from housing projects, with actual poor people and drug addicts and street criminals, and no website designers or young millionaires crowding the restaurants drinking martinis and recalling how much better it was before the dot-com-ers arrived. At last I was in America, the one I'd read about in books, where the gunshot crackled at night as patriotically as the exploding cymbals in our national anthem, and I felt real pride whenever someone was robbed on my block. If you were so materialistic as to own a car, it would be looted nightly as a welcome to democracy, and if the underclass really appreciated you, one of its members might select your backseat as a place to pass out. I rejoiced the night a friend's amplifier was stolen from his truck, and only after a series of interviews with the old men lurking in the doorways and an odyssey up a rickety back-alley stairwell was he able to buy the thing back for twenty bucks.

That year began a recession, and *The Wall Street Journal*

announced that job prospects were at their worst since the Great Depression, a statistic that instead of troubling me was cause for joy and drinking. My lure to the city was not to climb its gilded ladder of opportunity, but to sully myself in its gutters of temptation. And though not even the boom-ingest of economies and most lucrative of job offers would have induced me toward a sensible career, I celebrated the news of the bear market because it justified my not filling out applications and not attending interviews and not own-ing a pair of slacks. I found employment frying hamburgers and cheese steaks, and became, I guess you could call it, well known. Walking past the Oak Street projects the kids would yell Yo dude, where my french fries at? I think they meant it in a brotherly way.

So I set out looking for the Common Man, ducking first into the dive bars on Mission Street and taking a seat be-side those auto mechanics with tattoos and sideburns. I eavesdropped, hoping to hear plans for the next labor rally, or perhaps just some salty shop talk about the trouble with electronic fuel injectors.

"The English department at Brown was totally weak," said the one. "Half the profs couldn't even tell you what postmodernism was."

"Shoulda fuckin' majored in comp lit," said the other.

"Or gone to Yale."

They both snorted as if a funny joke had been told. Then the first mechanic ordered another dark ale, pulled a long chain from the pocket of his dungarees, and looked at a watch.

"Our boy with the X ain't gonna show."

"If all else fails we could score some H on Sixteenth Street."

"How déclassé would that be?"

This was all wrong: The hero of my adventure books could not be a faker, a privileged snit in a worker's costume. With sorrow I admitted that I was inadequate to be the leading man of my own books. If I wanted the author of my life story to resonate for generations with Hemingway and Jack London, I'd simply have to invent him. He would be a bit like me, of course, only less bookish and less sheltered, a man of the people and for the people. The Common Man. He would be rugged yet cosmopolitan, both American and continental, an empty template to be filled with my own robust experiences.

His name would be Travis LaFrance.

Proud of my creation, I slipped into a pair of high-heeled cowboy boots and went click-clacking down the city sidewalks looking for the high adventure and dangerous women that would become my hero's lifeblood. As if on cue, she appeared: Tania, in some bar, some night, a red-lipped lovely in leather pants sliding her fingers up my sleeve.

"I'm slap-happy," she said with a giggle. "I've been drinking wine since two in the afternoon."

I asked with whom and she said, "Just some man, just some old man." Then, laughing some more, she added, "It's my job, you know."

Soon I was in a car with her and a few other people, then in another bar where she chatted with some movie star she knew, ordered drinks, and at last tugged me out to the alley and pinned me to the brick wall and swallowed first my tongue then my lips and nose and finally my whole face, until the car idled close and went *beep beep* and she spit me out, took my phone number, and drove off into the night.

I stumbled away, assuming I'd never see her again, wishing I could revel in the thrill but instead calculating the quickly shrinking hours between now and my nine o'clock arrival at a downtown skyscraper where I would spend the day examining a file cabinet. To cultivate Travis LaFrance's rough-hewn blue-collar background, I had progressed from fry cook to housepainter. But the work was spotty and low-paying, and once the student loan bills began plunking in the mailbox, I decided Travis should examine the American office-place, if for no other reason than to resent it, and to long wistfully for open skies and callused hands. Following my peers like a lamb to the butcher, I signed up for some honest exploitation as a white-collar paper-pusher. I aced a battery of intelligence tests at one of San Francisco's bustling temp agencies, proudly demonstrating mastery of the English alphabet and twenty-five words per minute on the typewriter, thus qualifying for that bottom rung of office work, the envelope-stuffing and stamp-licking that in less enlightened eras was left to cretins and half-wits instead of holders of university degrees in English literature.

One day the phone rang. Sure enough, I'd been selected: Report first thing in the morning to the seventeenth floor of the Wells Fargo building, where I would "fill an assignment" as data entrist. I woke up early and reacquainted myself with such morning tasks as showering, shaving, brushing my hair, then donned my office uniform: the "dress pants" and "dress shirt" purchased five years earlier by my mother to make me presentable at high school graduation, her final contribution to my wardrobe, and quite likely the last brand-new garments I had acquired. Bedecked in a tie from my dad's closet and a pair of Red Wings from my grandfather, Travis LaFrance climbed aboard the mighty

Hayes 22 bound for the financial district, hoping no one would think he looked like a dork crossing the football field to fetch his diploma, but secretly thrilled and anxious to join the world of Work, to be a cog in the machine of free enterprise that rotates the planet. An adult, a man of means.

My infatuation with the workplace lasted twenty-six minutes. Checking in at Wells Fargo I was assigned a cloth-lined cubicle and a swivel chair, and there on my desk a computer blinked impatiently beside a big white cube of printouts, on whose every page were single-spaced lists of names and numbers. Who these people were or why they were on the list I was never told, never asked, never wanted to know. My job was to enter the data, then type:

P, RETURN, X, RETURN, A, RETURN

I looked up from my desk: dozens, hundreds, millions of souls doing this same thing, typing numbers, turning pages, moving mouses. How did they stand it? Why didn't they smash the equipment, cut wires, and piss on the carpet? If I was going to squander my citizenship in a democracy and imprison myself like this, go ahead and ship me to Siberia and cast me into the gulag, where at least the brisk cold would rub my cheeks and with a dull stick I could carve dissident verse on my bunk.

But instead of doing the only reasonable thing—kicking over my cubicle, ramming a fist through the monitor, lunging face-first through the plate glass and belly-flopping seventeen stories onto Montgomery Street—I held my position, maintained composure, and entered data. The longer my term in this cloth-lined cell, the sweeter the taste of freedom when I finally broke free.

Each day I kicked under the desk, clenching my toes, watching the clock until 5:30 came and I hauled ass down

the stairwell and into the fresh air, where I stuffed my tie
in my pocket, loosened my collar, and marched down Market Street. The first week I took the bus home, thinking
it the professional thing, but the rush-hour crowds were
more claustrophobic than the cubicle, so instead I walked,
splitting the gauntlets of crack salesman and porn-theater
barkers and European Moonies inviting me to a spaghetti
dinner, feeling the exhilaration of walking on my own feet,
of breathing in the crisp air even if it was heavy with exhaust, dodging the vomit and condoms and bums sprawled
on the sidewalk. By the time I turned on McCallister I was
tired and ready to catch the bus but was too cheap to pay
full fare for half a ride home, and at the end of my four-
week stint at Wells Fargo—they offered me a full-time job
but I stolidly declined—I'd worn holes in the leather soles
of my grandfather's wing tips.

So when I met Tania that night, I was about ready to
leave the city and go somewhere else, but I wasn't sure
Travis LaFrance had quite finished his apprenticeship in
the school of urban malaise. The next day it was hard to
concentrate on my work. By then I'd moved to a new assignment in another office, where on the first day they
showed me a wall of filing cabinets as long as a city bus,
and told me that my job was to open every file; those that
had been updated since 1990 were to be kept, the others
thrown away. By a small increment, this was a promotion
from data entry. Although the pay remained an even seven
per hour, I felt a bit more like my own boss here among the
files. No one watched me, and because this task had never
been done, no one knew how long it should take. And besides, with all the standing, bending, opening drawers, and

taking paces to the left or right, I was getting a bit more exercise than a swivel chair afforded.

I could hardly believe it, the next day, just as I walked in the door from my hour-long walk from work, when Tania called—yes, Tania!—and she wanted me to come over and maybe we'd see a movie. She lived on Fifteenth Street on one of the worst blocks in San Francisco, bordering the failing housing projects, alone in a third-floor apartment of a crumbling building. When I arrived she showed me black-and-white photos on the coffee table, most of her: naked, bound, blindfolded, with a man waving a pistol. She told me she had been a stripper until her kneecap popped out of its socket while she was onstage, and she had pushed it back and finished the number. Now she was writing a play and had been accepted to film school in New York, where she would be moving in the fall. She showed me a poster advertising her play, except that it didn't mention the title, venue, or date. It showed a platoon of women in leather, aiming machine guns and shiny revolvers, and in big block letters said, ARE YOU PREPARED?

By the time we got to the movie I was dizzy. The story involved a number of people being shot in the head then dumped into a quarry, all for a slightly humorous effect. It made me nervous. Walking home, Tania told me about a really nice friend who had bought her a computer, and who next month was taking her to the Bahamas. "The other night these guys paid me and my friend three hundred dollars to sit in a hot tub with them."

Back on her sofa, Tania sat on the toilet with the door open and peed, talking and laughing all along. I wondered what I had gotten myself into. Then she snapped her fingers and her clothes fell away and she slithered onto my lap, flicking her tongue into places I didn't know I had. She slid down my throat and coiled around my lungs, and just when she'd squeezed out all the air she reemerged in my fading vision and, waving her hand like a sorceress, commanded my clothes to unbutton themselves and lay down on the floor.

"You don't have any tattoos," she said. "I don't like tattoos."

All I could say was, "Neither do you."

She ran her fingers down her rib cage. "I can't pollute my moneymaker."

I knew that soon an enormous thug named Ramón would step from the closet or open the front door with a key and do terrible things to me. I had no way of knowing if I was being hustled. I had chanced into a world far from the lawns and campuses that I knew. She draped herself across me. I was scared. I was in trouble. Did I really think this nimble expert who gets paid for hot-tubbing was giving me a freebie, what, because she thought I was cute? Didn't I know she would demand a hundred dollars, or five hundred, or a thousand—I really had no idea how much things like this cost. I went along with it, though, for Travis's sake, knowing that someday he'd thank me. I was not afraid this pimp or bodyguard or whatever you want to call him would rob, beat, or kill me—these at least seemed noble hardships—but was stricken with worry that when they told me to pay up and I emptied the twelve dollars from my pockets, set it on the table with trembling hands, then the worst thing imaginable would happen: They would laugh at me.

But Ramón did not push open the door. When Tania

was done with me, she wanted to know how old I was, and I told her the truth, that I was twenty-two, but I don't think she believed it. She was twenty-four. She said that lately she'd had a thing for young boys, she didn't know why. She asked if I had a girlfriend and I said no, and after a while I asked if she had a boyfriend.

"I'm married," she said.

"Oh."

"But we have an open relationship. That was him in the picture you saw. With the gun."

"Right," I said. "The gun."

"Can you spend the night?"

"I guess," I said, then added that I had to be at work at 8:30, immediately regretting it. What kind of idiot would leave here for a day of filing at seven bucks an hour? I told her about the big wall of cabinets, sniffing with condescension to prove how far beneath me it was, but Tania just laughed.

"You're a Kelly Girl," she said. "That's cute."

All night I kept waking and wondering who would break down the door first: sneering Ramón with his brass knuckles or the cruel husband with his .357, but in the morning the sun shone through the lace curtains and I was still alive, and Tania kissed me good-bye and didn't ask for anything in return. That morning her town house door swung open on Fifteenth Street, and emerging from the birth canal was Travis LaFrance, a fully grown man. I stumbled into the bright light of Mission Street and made for the subway, wiping fluids from my face, smelling like the bedsheets of not just any woman but a professional. Here I was, San Francisco: the most swashbuckling Kelly Girl in the entire financial district. I had been born.

My days of astute file management were over. I stopped wearing my father's tie. I was careless. By the time I reached P in my alphabetical odyssey, I was hardly opening the files. I kept some and tossed others. I shredded the entire X section and a good part of Y, a sacrifice on the altar of Tania. And when I finished Z, the company was so impressed by my deft fingers and command of the alphabet that they, too, offered me a permanent position. I refused with a snort.

It was Travis LaFrance who now clipped down Market Street during the evening rush. A black man asked if I wanted to make ten bucks and I kept walking until he muttered behind me:

"White boy's afraid to talk to a black man."

I stopped. Travis LaFrance wasn't afraid of anything.

"You see," he began, smooth and well-rehearsed, "I lost the receipt for these things I bought at the Gap. Because I'm a black man, they won't give me my money back. But a well-dressed white boy like yourself won't have any problem. You get the money, and I'll let you keep ten bucks."

"It's a go," said Travis, snatching the bag from his hands. I marched down the sidewalk, pushed open the swinging doors, and plopped the merchandise on the counter.

"I want my money back," I announced.

The cashier reached into the bag. Then I realized, with some panic, that I hadn't bothered to see what was inside. She produced three identical pink ribbed-cotton tank tops. We both regarded the items speechlessly. Then I mumbled something about gifts for my sisters, which incidentally I don't have, and after a moment she rang open the cash drawer—I was, after all, a well-dressed white boy—and forked over forty dollars. I met my accomplice in the alley and gave him the money minus my commission, pleased with my work. Next time I'd ask for twenty.

Tania took me on a few dates. We "met for a drink," a new idea for Travis and myself, as we tended to soak ourselves in a bar until it closed. Now she named a place and I met her there. She drank chilled Bushmill's with no ice, and always paid the tab, wagging a finger and whispering about thrilling things outside of my world, like the club owner who every night would give her a thousand dollars from the till, just because, just to show how much he liked her. I offered to take her to dinner, but no, don't bother, she said, I'm not very hungry, but let's just go back to my place and I'll make you something. And her place smelled like old smoke and dried flowers, and there was no heat so we stood by the oven with the window open, and Tania boiled me a pot of macaroni and cheese, not Kraft, but the good kind, with the white not yellow cheese mix, the kind you get at a health food store.

"Here's what we'll do," said Tania, tousling my hair like I was her kid brother, and I couldn't tell if she was kidding. "I'll take you up to the Tenderloin and pimp you out, get a couple hundred bucks, and we'll take a trip somewhere." She told me her father was a lawyer and she'd been a good girl and done her homework until age fifteen when she discovered boys and left home; she had been living in bad neighborhoods ever since. Though she couldn't dance anymore, she still frequented the gentlemen's clubs, collecting gifts of scarves and jewels from the regulars.

She drove me here and there in a dented little hatchback that she always parked directly on the sidewalk at her front door but never got a ticket or, if she did, flung it immediately into the gutter. She left the windows open and the doors unlocked but nothing inside. Let them come in and look around, she declared, there's nothing to steal, just as long as they don't break the windows trying. One night we dropped by to see her friend, the one who took her to the Bahamas, in a big house on a winding road on a hill I didn't know, and Tania left me outside with the engine running while she delivered a brown grocery bag filled with I didn't ask what. It was better not to know. There I sat waiting once again for Ramón to emerge from the shadows with a small-caliber handgun and murder me point-blank: execution-style, as the *Chronicle* would report it the next day.

Then came the night of her play. I had told my housemate a little about Tania: She was an artist and a free spirit but beneath the tough facade was a sweet girl who harbored for me very special feelings. Of course I'd never brought her to my house; she might find the absence of derelicts asleep on the stoop to be hopelessly conventional. So I invited my housemate to the show, to witness firsthand the daring milieu in which I'd come to run.

We found the place among dark warehouses in an alley south of Market Street, somebody's house, a converted loft with a makeshift plywood stage and rows of folding chairs. The spectators wore fancy leather jackets and thick-rimmed glasses. None of us had any idea what we were in for. We paid our five dollars and found the last available seats. It was packed, standing room only, and when the lights went down Tania emerged onstage, high heels and a black gown, lips the color of blood, a cigarette and tall can of beer in one hand and the door money in a thick clump in the other. Tania thanked the crowd for coming and apologized for any trouble finding the venue.

"We were supposed to do the show in the Tenderloin, but the vice squad shut us down. So I'm glad you all found us."

She warned that the play would include nudity and was not advisable for the easily offended, and reminded this roomful of sophisticates that it was illegal to touch any of the girls.

"However, tipping is encouraged," she said, fanning the dollar bills. "And I have singles if you need change."

The play alternated between actual stripping and backstage scenes: conversations about the business, about drugs and money and freeloading boyfriends. Every now and again Tania came out to crack jokes and scold the crowd for undertipping, asking if we were having a good time. For the final scene, the girls hauled four people out of the front row onto the stage and arranged them around a table.

"A table dance?" the stripper said to the blushing participants. "Of course you can get a table dance!"

Then Tania reappeared, having swapped the fancy gown for thigh boots and a vinyl coat. She and a partner mounted the table and, toying with whips and crops, began to undress. Then something happened I will never forget. Tania bent over with her rear to the crowd, and her partner slipped on a latex glove and lubed it with clear oil, then one finger at a time began to probe up between Tania's legs until, wait, yes, really? She had the whole fist in there.

The audience's reaction is up for debate. I remember a stunned silence, but my housemate remembers hysteria and hollering and deciding it was time to move to a nice place like Iowa for graduate school. Tania, meanwhile, was giggling. Craning her neck to the audience, she made an announcement that I heard as intended just for me:

"Now you know what kind of girl I really am!"

And although my friend was impressed with my adventurous life when afterward in the alley Tania wrapped me in her leatherbound legs and smeared me with blood-colored kisses, my best memory of her was from a week later, a Sunday afternoon when she and I and her small-fisted friend drove up to Potrero Hill and sat in the grassy park and let a perfectly crisp and sunny San Francisco afternoon pass us by. Her friend brought her golden labrador and told me that when she finished college she might like to travel in Guatemala. We threw the tennis ball for the dog and snapped photos with a cheap camera. The sun was setting and the wind was cold and Tania leaned against me in the grass.

By then I had decided to leave San Francisco, to head to the desert where the falcons flew, not knowing that I would never move back or see Tania again. Now I was ready to leave. No, she hadn't stripped me of the innocence that shamed me; she'd stripped me of the shame. For Tania, innocence was not something to lose, but something to gain, a step toward the thing I really wanted: freedom. And when I tell you it was Tania who brought Travis to life, who freed me to be someone other than the person I was born, you might smirk and call me a fool, and speculate on her delusions and deceptions, but I will stand by her all these years later, because she knew that never mind what they say about privilege, the freedom some of us want is not at the top of the heap but the bottom, and I still smile when I remember her guns and fists and macaroni and cheese and think, yes, believe it: She was the first person I truly thought was free.

CHAPTER TEN

DESPITE MINGLING WITH THE TOREROS AND
sophisticates of Mexico City, I had yet to tap a community
of expatriate artists living the bohemian life. I knew that
while an American painting landscapes in Utah is a provin-
cial hack, the same guy brushing watercolors in Cuba or
France is a visionary. Just look at the Americans who flocked
to Prague after Communism. Rejecting the materialism of
their homeland, they emigrated to a place whose devastated
economy allowed them to pursue their art and eat daily in
cafés without ever getting a job. It was just like in Paris
in the twenties: another Lost Generation. And the poetry
slams and alternative rock groups that might have seemed
trite in American dormitories were, over there, the stuff of
a cultural awakening.

I myself, while studying in France, had made a pilgrim-
age to bohemia to join the New Lost Generation. I left Paris
so determined to be Lost that I carried neither guidebook
nor map. In Vienna I pantomimed my way onto a train and
finally emerged beneath the minarets of the great Eastern
capital that had beckoned my compatriots. I spent three
days in the bars and cafés trying to spark intellectual chats
with my Czech phrase book, but was surprised when none

*Driven by dreams of a record contract and a commercial
breakthrough, a Mexico City tunesmith grinds away at the
organ box.*

of the locals understood me and I couldn't find a single
American artist or poet. It wasn't until I met with the police kommissar to report the theft of my traveler's checks
and train pass that I learned the reason I wasn't feeling
swept up in the Prague Renaissance was because I was in
Budapest, Hungary. And though this detour snuffed my
dream of joining the New Lost Generation in the Czech Republic, it confirmed my own Lostness and inspired me to
one day visit a foreign country flush with Americans where
we could all be Lost together.

In Mexico City, messages from the publisher were arriving regularly demanding the dates I would be in Spain.
Having lived so richly for a month, I'd spent almost all the

book advance, and plane fare to Europe was out of the question. So I decided to find a Caribbean port town and gain passage across the Atlantic aboard a freighter. I had never been at sea, but I figured with my skills from the boatyard I could find work as a deckhand. I vacated my apartment and hefted my backpack to the bus station.

Colorful tourist posters advertised a dozen beach towns, and I inspected each carefully. So many options. Finally I decided on Zihuatanejo, partly because of the pretty pictures of palm trees and thatched-roof palapas, but mostly because I'd heard legend that it was a mecca for wandering expatriates such as myself. I took the overnight bus and awoke in a humid beachfront jungle.

First order of business after checking into a hotel was inspecting the wharf for an outbound freighter. However, all that I saw were yachts and fishing boats. I accosted a group of fishermen.

"¿Donde están los barcos grandes?"

"Where you go, amigo?"

"Madrid."

The fishermen looked at each other.

"Qué loco," said one.

"You like sportfish? We take you full day, we go half day. You catch good big fish, amigo. Special price."

"No, voy a España," I insisted.

"You need go aeropuerto, me friend."

"Quiero barco en el Atlántico."

"No es el Atlántico. Es Pacífico."

I looked at the sun dropping over the ocean. Technically, they were right.

"You come sportfish, guero. Catch big marlin, pay small price."

I returned to my hotel. The trip to the coast would not be a total loss if I could find some fellow American exiles.

But the next morning I found no cafés overflowing with artists. People alternated between sweating on lawn chairs lathered in sun oil and floating stupidly in the warm water. I watched the American couples wandering between snack carts and trinket stands.

"Honey, do you want to get a massage?" said he.

"I got a massage yesterday," said she.

"Let's find some shade."

"I don't think we're allowed under these umbrellas unless we're staying at this hotel."

"What if we pay?"

"We can probably pay."

"We could rent a boogie board."

"Or a snorkel set."

"Those hot dogs look good, wrapped in bacon."

"We'd probably get sick."

How dare they squander these precious hours abroad when they could be back in the shack making love or composing verse! It was decadent. The most exciting thing I saw any American do was strap on a parachute and get dragged around the harbor by a speedboat. If only Travis LaFrance were here with a woman. Struck by the muse, I sketched out a steamy Zihuatanejo exchange between Travis and a liberated expat:

> "It's hot out here," says she.
> "Let's go back to the cabana," says Travis.
> "We've been screwing ever since we got here."
> "I know."
> "Let's go in the water."

"Maybe we could rent snorkels and masks and do it underwater."

"I like the way you think," says she.

"Or we could rent one of these palapas for an hour and do it in there."

"What about some place we haven't already done it?"

"Let's go do it while being dragged around the harbor in parachutes."

"Do you think they'd allow us in the same parachute?"

"Maybe we'd each get our own parachute, and they'd drive the boats really close together. Like falcons mating in mid-flight."

"Wouldn't that be expensive?"

"I gotta spend this book advance somehow."

All the scene needed was a real female to flesh out the heroine a bit. In a burst of inspiration, I jumped up to go look at the girls.

Unlike Travis LaFrance, I really have no idea how to pick up a woman. I've never succeeded in thirty years. The only thing I know to say springs from my old-fashioned belief that you are what you do, so after five minutes I ask what she does. I pretend I'm asking out of innocent curiosity, that I'm not making judgments, but every time some girl says she works in marketing or website designing I get a small stomachache and, though I wish I could be as bighearted as Travis LaFrance and show her a good time anyway, what I actually think is what a stupid way to spend your life.

I wasn't going to settle for a dullard while researching the Zihautanejo love marathon. I wanted a girl like Tania, a free spirit and artist, who'd make the chapter tingle and zing. What's more, with the wisdom and experience I'd gained in the last decade, I figured I'd be better suited to satisfy Tania now than I was then. I was ready.

After a reconnaissance lap of the entire beach, I didn't see anyone like Tania. My only targets were a trio of plump American girls in swimsuits, accompanied by but clearly ignoring four husky collegiate boys knee-deep in the sea tossing a tennis ball. They were certainly on spring break from Somewhere State and had arrived in a group. The boys' horseplay and the girls' standoffishness told me two things:

1. The girls thought the boys were nice and before getting on the plane had considered "hooking up." But now they had decided the boys were total dorks, and though the girls would put up with their companions for the rest of the week they'd definitely take a better offer.
2. The boys' chances of getting laid, which on the airplane had seemed about 80 percent, were plummeting. They had taken to roughhousing, and within twenty-four hours they would stop acting nice, stop paying the drink tabs, storm off to the centro in search of a titty bar, and if they got drunk enough hire a whore.

Though these girls weren't exactly what I'd envisioned, the odds seemed good for the first lone wolf. But just as I was getting up to make my entrance someone signed up for a parasail ride and the operators flung it into the wind, and everyone had to dash away from the flying sand.

And then I saw a girl lying by herself with an unlit cigarette in her mouth. She had tattoos. She could well be a member of the New Lost Generation. I gave her a few glances trying to guess her nationality, and while she didn't exactly return them, neither did she look the other way, if you know what I mean. So once the parachute had launched I asked her for a cigarette. Neither of us had a light so I went scrambling through the cabanas on a search, finally lighting the thing off the cigar of a not-bad-looking woman sitting alone (stay on task, LaFrance: one woman at a time). When I returned the cigarette girl was gone, and after a quick panic I found her smoking in the shade with the trinket vendors, having found a light on her own.

When I sat down she was telling the vendor in broken Spanish that she'd been pickpocketed on the Mexico City subway. She was awaiting a bank card to arrive by FedEx, but the place she was camping didn't even have a street name or address. It was already two days late. My new prospect actually looked like Tania, with black hair and pale skin and a yard of tropical fabric wrapped around her tiny waist. She smiled easily, showing a mouthful of crooked teeth, and as she said something about a motorcycle accident and head trauma and a steady flow of insurance payments, she looked not so much like she'd been dropped on her head as a child, which was my first thought, but more like the hard years of experience had added character to a pretty face.

I soon knew all sorts of things about her. She'd been arrested in Coyoacan for smoking a joint on the street and had paid a bribe to get free. Her traveling companion was drunk all the time, sleeping it off right now in the tent.

He'd told her he might leave her because she was bad luck, but she thought her luck was fine, even though she'd also been arrested for weed back in San Francisco. Speaking of which, she was supposed to be in court today, but oh well, add Frisco to the list of places she couldn't go back to. She had three outstanding warrants in Minneapolis, too. Then she told me she'd been living in Venice Beach before coming to Mexico, working in North Hollywood, leading to my stock question, which is when the jackpot clanged and the lights flashed, because when I asked what sort of work she did in North Hollywood, without the slightest hesitation she said:

"Adult films."

"Let's get a beer," I said.

I followed her down an alley strung with ceramic fish and silver bracelets to a plastic table where meat was cooking and Cerveza Victoria was only eight pesos per bottle. Not seeing anywhere in her bikini where she might have money hidden, I paid for both beers. We sat down.

"I don't know, man," she said in a good Minnesota nasal accent. "When we came here seven years ago, these hotels weren't here. My friend lived in that house, so when we came this time, they let us camp there for thirty pesos."

She pointed at her tent, which was pitched in the shade of a boarded-up house. That was where her drunk companion was sleeping through his hangover. Ever since they got ripped off he'd been so negative all the time, she said. I asked when she'd had her motorcycle accident, and she said no, not her, it was her friend. We finished the beers.

"If I want any more I have to get money from the tent, man."

THE MAKING OF TORO

I nodded. Unlike Travis LaFrance, who always buys the
lady a drink, I didn't want to shell out another eight pesos
quite yet, partly because I didn't want her friend roaring
out of the tent with a crowbar and beating me silly, and
partly because I was cheap. She got up to fetch the money.

The man who emerged shirtless from the tent sat down
and shook my hand. He was tanned and dimpled, with hair
bronzed by the sun and matted in a heap, his good looks
struggling against red eyes and swollen face. He drank
from the quart bottle of beer she'd bought down the alley.

"I'm so fucking sick of this country," he said. "I hate it."

"I told you he was negative," she said, getting up from
the table.

"What's to be positive about? The first time it was
great, because we burned them. The next time it was good
until we got burned. Now this time it just plain sucks."

"Things are what you make of them." She walked away,
making a face that said it's no wonder we never make any
friends.

"I'm never coming back here unless . . ." he lit a cigarette. "Unless nothing. I'm never coming back here."

He looked at me as if he'd just remembered I was there.

"What's your deal, homey? Have enough money to buy
me a beer?"

I got up and bought another two beers. The man told
me that in addition to getting ripped off, the things he
hated about Mexico were the cold showers and having to
pay two pesos to take a piss. Things were fucked right now,
he said, but as soon as that bank card arrived they would
get better.

"If that doesn't work we'll find some scam. We always do."

They had hitchhiked here from Los Angeles, via Mexico City, and now he planned to hitch back to Florida.

"I'm going to Miami, where I can fuck for money."

The girl had been wandering in circles and now, apparently realizing there was nowhere else to go, returned to her chair. Until then I hadn't learned their names. I told them I was Travis LaFrance and the man said his name was Jack Shaft.

"I'm Kumelia," said the girl. "With a K."

I had a suspicion those weren't their real names, but I didn't let on. It is not uncommon for an American once he's stepped on foreign soil to shed his cocoon and flitter about as a new person with a new name. Jack Shaft told me that in his line of work they earn two thousand dollars for a one-hour scene.

"Good money as long as I don't bust a nut."

"Even if you do bust a nut," said Kumelia, thoughtfully.

"Then it just takes a little longer. They don't care, as long as I don't get shy. Sometimes Kami gets shy, but that's all right, because she's the girl. Without the man, there's no show. There's no money shot. And without the money shot—"

"Then it's art," I suggested.

Jack Shaft snorted. Weren't we a trio of hard-living expatriate artists! And in fifty years young writers will pass on legends about how in the hungry years before we were famous Jack Shaft and Kumelia and Travis LaFrance used to hang out together in cafés in Zihuatanejo. I called for another beer. We were getting along great.

"Did you hear what he said? Without the cum shot, it's art, yo."

"It can be art anyway," said Kumelia. "Manuel said some of my still shots were artistic."

"Who the fuck is Manuel?" demanded Jack Shaft.

"In Minneapolis," she said.

Jack Shaft raised an eyebrow to tell me I didn't have to believe her bullshit if I didn't want to. He sucked from the big brown bottle.

"I always had this dream of doing porn. I knew I'd be good at it. So every girlfriend I had, I asked her to do it with me, on film, but they always said no. And I always said if you won't do it I'll find someone who will. Then finally I met Kami."

"That's not how it was, man. You never said that to me."

"Then why'd you do it?"

"Because," she said, snatching the beer and drinking, "I sort of wanted to."

"Right." He took back the beer. "Give me a cigarette."

"At first I'm shy," she said. "But then I forget the camera is there and start to enjoy it. Also the money helps."

Jack Shaft told me their ultimate plan: Forget about films, the Net was where it's at. They wanted their own website, and they'd broadcast themselves live from around the world, having sex in exotic locations. Their subscribers would get an e-mail: "Log on at ten o'clock to see Jack Shaft and Kumelia fucking on the beach in Tahiti, or in a boat, whatever." The money would be automatically deposited in their account, and with an ATM card they'd withdraw whatever cash they needed to continue traveling. "One thing I want to do is go to the busiest intersection in a huge city—New York, Minneapolis, Seattle—and at the stroke of noon, when everyone comes out of their skyscrap-

ers for lunch, fuck her real hard for one minute, right there
on the street, live on the Net."

All they needed was a digital camera, a laptop, and a cell
phone. Like Travis LaFrance they would see the whole
world, hump in it, and get paid. Jack Shaft and Kumelia
were doing things on their own terms. Their art was their
life, and versa vice.

"But I don't even have money for my next drink. What
about you, homes? Got any money you want to get rid of?"

"Hardly. I've only got ten thousand pesos left of my
book advance."

He gave a sidelong look at Kumelia.

"About ten thousand more than us." He spoke as if he'd
heard the lines in a movie and now wanted to try them out
himself. "When I was a drug addict, I was good at it. Now
I'm a drunk. And I'm good at it. All I do is drink, and sleep,
and then my girlfriend wakes me up to give me a beer."

"Maybe you could be more positive."

"I positively have to take a leak," he said and got up.

Kumelia and I sat there smoking.

"One of these times I won't be here. I'll find someone
better."

"Don't you like it here?"

"I liked it last night. When everyone was gone except
for the children, and they ran around and laughed. That
was my favorite part."

"Where do you want to go next?"

"Somewhere peaceful. That's all."

She asked me about my book. Kumelia was really inter-
ested in my craft, and wanted to know all about a writer's
life: how much I got paid, what I did with the money, and

whether I used traveler's checks or cash or ATM. When Jack Shaft returned from the toilet she said:

"Travis was telling me about his book."

"I should write a book, yo, of all the fucked-up situations I've been in."

"That could be the title," she said. *"All the Fucked Up Situations I've Been In."*

"I was always told that the end was coming so I'd better watch out. But the world's not ending. Fuck that. There's no tomorrow. My tomorrow is right now."

"Right on," I said.

"Go get me another beer, baby."

She hesitated long enough to let us both know she wasn't his servant. Once she was out of earshot, Jack leaned in close.

"I think she likes you, homes."

"What?"

"She ain't my girlfriend if that's what you're thinking. Fact is, I've been wanting to ditch her."

"Howcome?"

"She hasn't done anything for two years but follow me around and make porn and freeload off my disability."

He lit another cigarette.

"Ask her out to dinner. Let's cook up some plot to get me out of here, and then you can keep her. Where you staying, anyway?"

I told him the name of my hotel. "But I'm leaving tomorrow."

"Here's your damn beer," said Kumelia.

"Travis was telling me he's gonna split tomorrow. We should all take a road trip together."

"Who has a car? And you're welcome."

"I bet homey could rent one."

"I could totally rent one. We could go find some beaches."

"Wouldn't a beach be nice, Kami?"

"I'd like that."

What an adventure! So we arranged to meet at my hotel in the morning, and after another drink I headed back across the bay. I found a taqueria and ate by myself. I chewed slowly and asked for a second strawberry soda and watched a soap opera on the television. Then I walked back to the hotel hoping people would be drinking beer and talking revolution on the patio, but instead it was dark and everyone had gone to sleep. I paced back to my room and lay wide awake on the cot. I watched spiders on the ceiling. Just a few hours separated from the reckless sex-artists, and I already missed them. So I put on my shoes and walked up the cobblestone alley. Jack Shaft had told me about a liquor store where they went to drink cane liquor. Sitting on the steps were a couple of Mexicans I'd seen on the beach.

"Where you friends, gringo?"

"I was about to ask you."

"We seen the chava. She a bad chava."

"You saw them here?"

"She want the mota but she no give the pucha."

"When did she leave?"

"Ten cuidado, dude. Mucho cuidado."

I stepped inside to buy a popsicle, and the men on the steps kept talking. My language skills had improved to where I could understand the words, but it took me a moment to translate.

"Lo va a chingar."

"Pendejo quiere perder su dinero."

"Y por una puta."

I bid them buenas noches and clopped down the road, repeating the words over in my head until finally with a swelling of pride I figured their gist: I was going to get ripped off. That's what they said anyway, but what did they know? What's the point of learning a new language if all you hear is lies?

In the morning Jack Shaft and Kumelia arrived early with their backpacks. I suggested some food before renting the car. I led them through the streets to find tacos. When the taqueria was closed, Jack Shaft decided to get drunk. For six pesos he found a plastic bottle of pure cane rubbing alcohol that he mixed in a plastic cup with Pepsi. He sat there on the steps of the liquor store stirring with his finger, then finally took a sip, gagged, and swallowed it down. Kumelia made a retching face: It had come to this. The strain of being in exile was showing on Jack Shaft, but I trusted that his work on camera justified his personal shortcomings.

In the restaurant they poured a bit of the alcohol on a spoon and set it on fire. Kumelia poured the flaming drops onto the floor and they laughed. Jack Shaft told me they used to work for a big Internet sex company, but he got fired for drinking all the time.

"How's the money in that?" I said.

Jack Shaft shrugged. "Two bills for a two-hour session."

"Two thousand bucks." I let out an admiring whistle.

"Two hundred," he corrected me.

"I miss it," said Kumelia. "As soon as you're done you get a hundred e-mails saying how good you were, or how turned-on you made someone. Usually they're writing you from work."

"They like it because it's interactive. Someone will e-mail and say fuck her in the ass and the cameraman gives me the word and I do it."

"Films are better money," said Kumelia, "but I don't like films as much. When you're done, it's like: two people clapping."

"We don't do it for the money."

"Neither do I," I said.

I was trying to block out the warning the men had given me at the liquor store and to regain the moment of down-and-out artists talking craft. These were the moments a writer dreams about. Kumelia ate her eggs and tortillas. Jack Shaft drank the rubbing alcohol and Pepsi.

"Go pay the bill, baby. And get me another soda."

"Sit. Heel. That's what you sound like."

"And roll over. Just get me a fucking Pepsi, yo."

Once she was gone he said: "She wants you."

When Kumelia returned with the Pepsi, Jack Shaft mixed it with his finger and talked about people he'd burned, cashing bad checks and taking a cut from coke deliveries.

"I'd never pull a bitch move like pickpocketing. That's how those punks did me. I'd sooner shove a gat in a motherfucker's face."

And though we were getting along fine, I couldn't shake the feeling that someone was about to get burned. Their being two and my being one, combined with my having money and their having none, made it likely that the person getting burned would be me. I wished Travis LaFrance was here. He wouldn't get burned. He's one of them. The Common Man doesn't steal from the Common Man.

"I'm a porn star, yo. I can do whatever I want."

"Manuel thinks you're a loser," said Kumelia.

"That bitch thinks I'm a loser?"

"Everyone thinks you're a loser. Even your mom."

"Well, they can all suck my cock."

"Your own mother?"

"And your mother, too."

"That's disgusting, man."

"It is disgusting that they'd do it," crowed Jack Shaft, grimacing to hold down another sip. "And then I'd puke on their shoes."

I didn't have what it took to be an expatriate like Travis LaFrance. If I was a true bohemian I'd just go with my whim, follow the dangerously alluring girl, and if they took my money, fine, I shouldn't be so attached to it in the first place. But as much as it shamed me, I saw at that table that I was inexcusably materialistic, too selfish to support the gypsy life. I got up and said I had to check out of the hotel.

"When are you getting the car?"

"I'll be back in ten minutes."

I paid my portion of the bill on the way out, then sprinted down the alley. I was breathing hard. I pulled my bags onto the street and hailed a cab. I sank low in the backseat in case Jack Shaft and Kumelia were in the streets looking for me, and I sank even lower in case the eyes of literature were on me, witnessing the supposed adventure writer sneak away from his fellows hidden in a taxi.

"Terminal de camiónes," I told the man, and we rattled down the cobblestone and out of town.

CHAPTER ELEVEN

MEXICAN BULLFIGHTING WAS IN TROUBLE. City officials had discovered that bulls killed in the Plaza Mexico were less than the required four years old and had had their horns blunted to protect the toreros. The taurine writers moaned that the corrida was dead or at least dying, blaming the impresarios for greed, the ganaderos for poorly bred cows, the matadors for cowardice, the fans for ignorance, the press for backstabbing, or the government for meddling in the world of toros, which answers to no authority but God. While Spain was in a bullfighting renaissance, Mexico was in a slump. Most papers agreed that there was only one real figura in Mexico right now: El Zotoluco.

So when I read that he would be in Texcoco the day before Easter, I returned to Mexico City. I barely had money to get home, to say nothing of a jaunt to Spain, but I would end this trip with a bang, perhaps two ears and a tail. A stirring account of El Zotoluco's magic would not just win the lost faith of my publisher, but also reaffirm the faith of a Mexican people doubting their own fiesta. Imagining all the young toreros in the future who would thank Travis LaFrance for rescuing their pastime from the dustbin of obsolescence, I fired off a note to New York.

MINOR CHANGE TO TORO'S SUB-SUBTITLE STOP INSTEAD OF
AFICIONADO'S ODYSSEY FROM TIJUANA TO MADRID I PREFER
AFICIONADO'S ODYSSEY FROM TIJUANA TO MEXICO CITY AND
BACK STOP MORE POETIC STOP ALSO WILL APPEAL MORE TO
OUR TARGETED AUDIENCE OF WESTERN HEMISPHERE READERS
STOP ABRAZOS TRAVIS

*Travis: I don't understand the logic of your suggestion, but we
can discuss the title once we get to Madrid. Please send your flight
number and date. —Ed.*

NEGATIVE STOP MY STORY IS HERE STOP ABRAZOS TRAVIS

I then walked down the street to a travel agency, priced
the Spain tickets for the last time, then booked a flight to
Los Angeles on Easter Sunday, three days away.

On Thursday I take a series of trains and peseros through
the outskirts of Mexico City to scope out the scene. Out in
the grasslands trash burns and carcasses rot and the kids
on the bus pinch their noses, and we arrive finally in Texcoco at the International Festival of the Horse.

I wander the fairgrounds with my mouth agape. Roller-
coasters and dancing horses, donkey rides and a mechanical
bull, get your picture taken on an ox. I am paralyzed like in a
television store where you can watch all the channels at once.
Mariachis are muted by disco blaring from refrigerator-size
speakers. I see the hairless bodies of goats heaped in a
wheelbarrow and pushed through the throngs, then pulled
from their skins and crucified on an open flame. I watch men
climb a big tall pole and play their flutes and do that famous
Mexican thing where they tie themselves to a rope and come
spinning down to the earth.

In my palsy I miss the bullfight. But that's all right because Saturday I'll see El Zotoluco—El Zotoluco!—the only one brave enough to execute LaFrance's revival of the corrida, and tomorrow I'll see El Enanito, whose name I don't recognize but who is surely a good torero, too.

So that night I go to the cockfight instead. Surely *Toro* could use a detour into another bastion of Mexican manhood. I'm frisked at the door by cops in camo and pay one hundred pesos for a seat in the high part of the steep concrete ring over a circle of dirt quartered with chalk. Everyone is shouting and drinking and smoking and waving money at their chicken. I expect an advanced betting method, electronic maybe, but no: To place a bet you whistle and holler at the bet-girls down in the ring, who smile efficiently like stewardesses in navy blazers and peach blouses and name tags. With your fingers you gesture how much you want to bet and then they write it on a paper scrap that they stuff in a slit tennis ball and chuck your way. Half the time it beans your head or knocks over your drink. The girls throw pretty well, but if you're up here in the cheap seats they might hand it off to one of the guys in suits that huddle like stock traders in the pit and let him lob it up instead.

The man sitting next to me is betting lots of money, ordering rum drinks two at a time. He opens his cigarette box and offers me one, Marlboros stacked neatly on one side and Salems on the other. He tells me his girlfriend lives in the United States. He explains how everything works down in the pit. The first fight starts: a few seconds of squawking and slashing. Don't worry if someone stands up and blocks your view, the fight is simulcast on televisions hung from the rafters. If you ever thought a boxing referee in his bow tie dwarfed by the giant black fighters looked a bit overdressed and self-important, wait till you see a grown man with a gray toupee and three-piece suit break up two chickens, then, with a hand tucked behind his back, bark out a ten-count.

The chickens just lie there waiting to die. It's sort of boring. Whichever is panting fastest is closest to death, my friend tells me. He's getting drunk, starting to breathe fast himself. Am I married, he wants to know, and what's the name of my hotel?

Meanwhile, each dying bird has a designated handler, sort of like a coach, who picks up the chicken and performs rescue breathing. Blowing under the tail feathers and massaging the legs, he readies the contender for another round. The handlers are cold and professional; I wonder if they mourn for their chickens. My friend orders me a beer and tells me he'd love to take me to a bullfight. He asks if I have a car and offers a lift back to Mexico City.

Muerte! Muerte! shouts the crowd.

Then my friend puts his hand on my knee and the ref declares one cock the winner. Somebody sweeps up the feathers and rakes away the blood as the betting begins again. The hand is still on my knee. Maybe it's some gesture of aficionado's kinship that I am narrow-mindedly misinterpreting. This wouldn't happen to Travis LaFrance. My friend winks and I finish my beer. I hop up and say I'll be right back, but instead hurry toward the exit, hearing a last cockadoodledoo in the smoke-filled corridor as I make my way out.

The next day is Good Friday. I go to the suburbs of Mexico City to see the Last Supper and the betrayal by Judas reenacted on a stage. I get on a bus where portraits of Christ and the Beatles hang over the windshield, and I ask the driver if this line takes me to Jesus. He isn't sure but thinks I might have to transfer.

The father of a family in the back of the bus assures me I'm in the right place. "Puedes venir con nosotros," he says. So he and I and his wife and kids get off the pesero and walk through a police traffic blockade along an avenue past a reeking industrial fish market. The whole world is going to see Jesus, and we dodge between cars parked on the sidewalk and policemen blowing whistles and vendors selling trinkets of the Son and the Virgin.

Then the crucifixion parade. Robed Arabs wear glued-on beards and red Roman soldiers pull pit bulls on short chains. Buglers ride horseback, ladies don finery, and Jesus in rags gazes serenely into the TV cameras with thorns on his head as the trumpets sound and drums beat. Behind the savior, lady cops on four-wheelers smoke cigarettes. Lastly plods a guy bearing a pink cross of cotton candy.

And it occurs to me that this chapter won't simply jump-start Mexican bullfighting, it will resurrect it. The crucifixion will provide perfect background images. But when I learn Jesus will take three hours to reach Calvary I bid good-bye to my host family and jump on a bus for my ringside appointment with El Enanito. I can invent the Christ images, but I can't afford to miss another bullfight. I arrive late in Texcoco, buy my ticket, and rush to a seat.

Something is very wrong in the bullring. A she-midget in pink tights and a spangled silver blouse is lip-synching a mambo. A full-sized clown does the chicken walk. Another midget emerges in a bear suit, followed by one in a dalmatian suit, then a leopard and a rabbit and a female dressed like a hen, and they dance about merrily, getting whistled and booed, the fiction of the lip-sync collapsing when the dalmatian kicks the singer and she pegs him with the mike. I sense real anger and am not convinced they're acting.

The crowd cheers, mostly children. Where are the bulls, where are the bullfighters? God, is it hot here, the midday sun pummeling us all, people ducked under umbrellas and backed against the wall. There's no shade. I flip through my dictionary and discover that enanito means midget. I tell the beer lady to keep it coming.

Now here comes the bull—well, a calf actually—and a midget dressed as a bunny rabbit dances the mambo. The big people tug tail and grapple horns while the little people take running dives beneath the calf's belly. An announcer says something over the speakers, but it's muffled and lost in feedback. Then it's over. I feel sullied. As we file out of the bullring I'm drunk and depressed and don't know what to do next.

But what's this? Flamenco dancers! I duck into the Café Olé Olé and drink more beer and watch the women dance, three of them with white skin and black eyes and red Spanish dresses. A gypsy sings with a lisp and a boy slaps a wooden box with his bare hands. Nobody complains one bit when the dancers' dresses float up past their thighs. Oh, and especially the one with the flat hat and the rose behind her ear, is she smiling at me? This is a woman who could make you think she loved you, even if she didn't. It occurs to me in a flash that in *Toro* she will be Spanish and will love the corrida, and I'll invite her to come sit with me—better yet, she'll have complementary barrera seats—and we'll drink sangria and fall in love and talk about Sevilla. "Resurrection in Texcoco" will prove that you don't have to go to Spain to see fine bulls and fine flamenco or, for that matter, to write a book about it.

When I approach the dancer after the show, she's not from Spain at all, but from Mexico City. I ask if she's an aficionada and she says though she admires the dancelike movement of toreo, overall she thinks the killing is cruel and never goes to see it.

"But I dance here every day. Will you come see me tomorrow?"

"I promise."

I take the bus back to my hotel and watch TV. I'll be fresh and impressionable for tomorrow when I get to see El Zotoluco kill and Latecia dance.

As you know from *Toro*, El Zotoluco stunned us all in Texcoco, cutting three ears and restoring his countrymen's faith in the bullfight. Remember that as I crossed the Zócalo to catch the metro, pilgrims were already gathering for the all-night Easter revival. Believers hoisted statues of Jesus and Mary onto their shoulders and marched in from the outlying churches, setting the tone of holy carnival that would carry over to the artistry in the ring. But here I must admit that my stirring description of El Zotoluco's faenas was sort of a fake. I copied and translated it from an online newspaper the next week.

The day I go to see him, things do not go right. As soon as I get off the bus a rainstorm bursts over Texcoco, and wearing only shirtsleeves I buy a plastic poncho for ten pesos. By the time I rush through the ticket gate and sprint to the restaurant I am soaked. The cook pops an umbrella over the flames that lick a spit of pork. I am here an hour early, just in time for the three o'clock flamenco.

The rain falls down on Olé Olé, hammering the fiberglass roof and dripping onto the floor where a busboy pushes the puddles with a broom. All tables are occupied except those under the leak, and the waiters drag them to a dry place. They seat me behind the stage, where I can watch the dancers with their hair pulled taut, putting on lipstick, smoking cigarettes, sometimes clapping hands or clicking a heel on the concrete. Isn't my Latecia fabulous, dressed the way a dancer should, with a black tank top and tight crisp jeans and scarf tied in her hair? The rain leaks onto the plywood dance platform and the manager lays out some cardboard. Latecia sees me and smiles, then they all file into the rest room and return in ruffled dresses.

The music starts. The performers are crammed beneath a pair of crossed banderillas and a plastic sign for tortilla flour. It's packed in here, wet and humid, and I wonder if a spotlight will short or a dancer will slip. One of them hauls a man onstage to dance with her, and he's nervous, but those damn Mexican men, they all seem to know how to dance and he pulls it off just fine. Just as I'm thinking, better him than me, here comes Latecia in her flat hat, swishing her skirt and pounding her heels, and what's this? seeking me out! I breathe. I'm afraid, but then: I'm Travis LaFrance, ladies' man, so I follow her up to that wooden stage in front of all those people and clap my hands and stomp my boots. She dances close enough so I can feel her breath on my neck. It seems passable, or at least nobody laughs loud enough for me to hear, and it rains and rains and rains and rains, more water in fifteen minutes than there's been in two months. The bucket on stage is overflowing onto the cardboard and the busboy trots out the push broom between songs. Men shout *Granada! Sevilla! Torero! Sevilla!* over the drumming of the rain and the drumming of the drum and the flick of the fingers on the guitar and the snappety-snap of high heels on plywood, and so many people are pinned to tables smoking cigars and drinking rum that the roof will either burst from inside or collapse beneath the rainfall.

But now it's over and I need to go to the stupid bull-fight, when what I really want to do is sit here in Olé Olé and court Latecia, and besides that it's pouring rain. But a job is a job, so I head out into the storm and buy my general admission ticket, telling myself to cheer up, after all, it's El Zotoluco. When I reach the gate everyone is streaming out. What's happening? I ask. Oh joy, the bullfight is rained out! I rush back to the restaurant and search for my dance partner with nothing else to do for the entire afternoon. But then: I shouldn't be joyful. I just botched all my opportunities to see a bullfight in Texcoco, and I have a plane ticket to Los Angeles tomorrow, and now I'll never see El Zotoluco. I've failed completely to be an adventure writer. But there's Latecia drinking a bottle of water, and I sit down and everything is fine. I'll make up some shit for the book later, I think, as she tells me she's been a dancer all her life, modern and ballet, but now that she's reached thirty she does mostly flamenco because, she pauses, her body and mind finally understand it.

"I feel it with all my being," she says.

"I feel it, too."

She says that for the other kinds of dance she performs at a good theater instead of a cheap restaurant with a plywood stage, but there's better money in flamenco than in art. And besides, the theater audiences are old and dull. I ask if she likes it when the people hoot and catcall, and she admits she does. She's danced in New York and Paris, and I pretend to be a knowledgeable American, dropping names of streets and places in New York I've never been to, and just as I'm about to propose buying her a plane ticket to Utah she spares us the embarrassment by mentioning her husband.

All is not lost, right? We can still be friends and I won't mention the husband in *Toro*. We eat lunch, and I'm crushed by the double failure of missing the most important bullfight of my book and not eloping with a flamenco dancer, and I'm kept up late that night, my last night in Mexico, by the all-night Easter eve celebration in the Zócalo, by the converted and the hopeful, and lying open-eyed in the hotel bed I see that all I've wanted was to make my life a good story, to be the star of my own book, but now it's clear that mine has no plot, no arc, is just a series of anecdotes and a string of scenes sitting in stands watching the performers perform, not a hero but a spectator, and the only good parts are the parts I make up. And while I lie here thinking, they're outside living, thousands of Christians deep into Jesus, singing songs of resurrection and shouting yes and crying to the world that they believe, we believe, we've really found something in which we believe.

CHAPTER TWELVE

———

TORO WAS TRANSCENDING THE DOGMATIC
confines of the original proposal into the realm of rare vision. Returning north of the border, LaFrance snares a so-
phisticated babe in the Slovak photojournalist, Hannah
Kjoprczak. As they barrel from Los Angeles toward Tijuana
in his pickup truck, she tells of her hungry years in the
Prague underground and how her critiques of U.S. imperialism have made it difficult to get working papers in this
country. She speaks good English with a sexy accent. Her
clothes are dark, simple, feminine, stylish: no name brands.
Perhaps she sewed them herself. In Orange County she
glares across the freeway lanes at the fake Spanish roofs of
tract houses.

> "And this," she sniffs, "you Americans call this
> freedom."
> "Stucco prisons," says Travis LaFrance.
> "If you take away the terra-cotta and the—how
> do you call it?—garbage incinerator, it is the same as
> a coal miners' barracks in my grandparents' village."
> "There's still freedom left in this country," says
> Travis LaFrance, "but you gotta walk two days from
> the end of the road to find it."

"Will you take me there, Travis?"

"Of course I will."

LaFrance twists up a cigarette one-handed and tells her the story of how he once snared a cougar cub with some twine he'd fashioned from a yucca.

"For what do the Americans always kill an innocent?" says Hannah.

"I pulled a cactus spine from its paw," says Travis patiently. "Then I let it go."

The erotic tension between this brainy dissident and our laconic cocksman is forcefully rendered throughout the final chapters of *Toro,* as primal as the dance between man and bull, reaching a conclusion equally lyrical and inevitable atop the starched white sheets of Los Amantes Motor Lodge in downtown El Centro.

Some of it is fiction. Sure she has a Slovak last name, but she's never been there and doesn't speak the language. Hannah is from Detroit. She's not precisely a photojournalist, though she does work in a darkroom and owns several cameras. She lives in L.A., across the street from my friend Henry, and when he introduced us one night she said she was working on her portfolio and wanted to take pictures of a bullfight. Isn't America a fine country! Here the women volunteer to go to the bullfight, and you don't even have to ask them.

Her offer couldn't have come at a better time. I was down to my last two hundred dollars, hiding out from the publisher at my parents' house and not responding to his messages. Though I knew my work in progess was a thing of grandeur, I worried that its bold genius might elude certain pedantic editors. What it required was a dramatic cli-

max to wring sobs and cheers from even the most anemic
New York automaton. Then in walked Hannah, on the eve
of a Tijuana bullfight.

"I'll show you sights your camera could never imagine,"
I told her. "Wear something you can get dirty."

But then I realized I'd screwed everything up and it
was too late to change. The day before, in a terrible lapse
of judgment, I'd invited my parents to come with me to
Tijuana. Having squandered my advance on sushi, I was
camped out in their spare bedroom. I wish I could say I invited them in order to spend good family time, but actually
I was just dreading an all-day drive to sit alone through the
deaths of six bulls, and couldn't find anyone else to go, and
if you really need to know how low I'd sunk, I hoped they'd
buy me lunch.

So on Sunday morning when the Slovak photojournalist
arrives at my parents' house in an old VW bug, I'm trembling. I try to think up ways to impress upon her that I am
not only a legitimate writer but also a romantically available adult man who, for reasons temporary and insignifi-
cant, happens to be staying at his parents' house. Isn't she
lovely! I sense right away she's different from Travis's other
girls: She's the real thing. For one, she speaks English. For
another, she actually knows my name and is willingly coming on a date with me.

But everything is wrong! What kind of adventure writer
takes his parents along on the first date? Travis LaFrance
never even sees his parents. That would be bourgeois. He
never had a childhood, certainly not in the suburbs. He
strode in to this world as a fully grown man with a mustache on his lip and a working-class chip on his shoulder.

But my parents could never understand Travis LaFrance. How could I tell them I wished I had different parents without hurting their feelings? So I say nothing and let them embarrass me. They're out in the front yard with their walking shoes and water bottles, and as soon as Mom sees Hannah's Volkswagen she remembers the one just like it she had when she got married.

"It was my dowry! And it broke down half a mile from the church."

A reminiscence of the wedding and honeymoon ensues as we all board the sedan and speed down the San Diego Freeway. I'm driving and Mom and Dad are in back. I shoot Hannah a cool sidelong glance that says I'm not necessarily related to those people back there and maybe we can ditch them at the border and sneak off together, but she doesn't catch its meaning. By now they're peppering her with questions: Mom asks about Mexican villages Hannah has visited, Dad wants to know what classes she took in college.

We continue toward Orange County. I prepare to say something snide about this stronghold of gated privilege and narrow-mindedness. I know that as an artist I should hate the place, and I pray Mom and Dad won't mention to the photojournalist that my grandparents lived down here in a retirement village. A hero like Travis LaFrance is not allowed to have spent any of his childhood at Leisure World.

We're on the same freeway we used to drive on Sundays to visit Meema and Peepa, Dad always driving, Mom in front, Richard and I in back of the Datsun wagon with stained vinyl smelling like sour milk. We stuck our heads out the window, waiting giddily for the moment when we rolled over the gatehouse speed bumps and Richard hollered to the fogey in a police-looking uniform, Hey mister, where's your gun? It was a fine thing to say, and I imagined the guard awaited it all month as eagerly as we did. Peepa was so proud when we told him about it that he drove Richard back to the guardhouse just to hear him say it again: Hey mister, where's your gun?

Back then I didn't know I shouldn't like Leisure World. We would go to the mall or the matinee or the fields by the freeway and buy strawberries by the basket, and ask if we could go to SafariLand, but we never could because it closed down after that lady got her head bitten off. Meema and Peepa took us to swim in the Clubhouse pool, then we changed into dry clothes and cranked swimsuits through the wringer and watched the water splash onto the concrete and evaporate in a whiff of chlorine. We played a round of shuffleboard, shaking grains of wax over the green cement and whacking those little pucks, my brother and I, at dangerous speed, sending them caroming into the neighboring lanes of disapproving seniors. At dinnertime we went to Coco's or Sizzler for the early-bird special or, if it was a birthday, the Velvet Turtle, where the napkins were folded in fancy shapes on the tablecloth. When the check arrived Dad said, Let me, but they would never let him, and they bickered before Dad gave up and Peepa paid the bill.

On Thanksgiving we stayed home in the condominium, where blue porcelain plates hung on the wall and the carpeting was white and a big wooden clock chimed every half-hour. Black olives lay between celery spokes in round crystal plates, and Meema snuck us as many sodas as we wanted, even if Dad said only one. Peepa in a golf shirt went to the back bedroom and plinked a few notes on his xylophone. He'd come to California from Rock Island, Illinois, and graduated in the first class at Hollywood High

School and worked in his parents' grocery store on Sixty-second Street, where one day he met Meema when she was still Charlotte. She was from Kansas, and they lived all their lives in Los Angeles, where Dad was born, and then after the riots moved with all their friends to Leisure World, where the streets were clean and the buildings brand-new. They played golf and bridge, and he joined the Jolly Boys and she was a candystriper at El Toro General. If anyone rang the doorbell Meema sang yoo-hoo, and after dinner Peepa gave us each a dollar, and we drove home on the free-way, sleeping in the way-back, and even with my eyes closed I recognized the off-ramp and the turns and hills and street-lights as we approached our house, and I would keep them closed so Dad would carry me inside to bed.

You had to be fifty-two to live in Leisure World, and I knew that as soon as my parents were eligible they would move in, and I calculated that in just forty-six years I could get my own apartment on Via Something-or-other, be-cause, really, who wouldn't want to live there? We'd all be together and wouldn't have to bother with the one-hour freeway drive; when we wanted to go to the Clubhouse, we'd just hop in the golf cart and scoot right over.

As my parents and I drive to Tijuana it's the first time we've come this way together in ten years. Now I'm driv-ing. The car is nicer, smooth and air-conditioned and quiet with the windows closed. The seats are leather. Mom and Dad are in the back. They're old now. They don't look or act old, but it's a fact: They're sixty-two and have a grand-daughter. Mom had a carcinoma removed and Dad has a pacemaker. Some of their friends have already died.

Mom and Dad never moved to Leisure World. I now know that you don't want to live with your parents, even if you like them. Peepa would come to our house and check that all the windows were locked and comment that Dad's car needed a wash. Some parents don't want their kids to grow up, my Dad told me, after his had died. I saw what he meant.

Meema died first, and Peepa lasted a few months. He was eighty-one years old, learning to fry eggs and balance the checkbook, but a few nights after we moved him into a home he just went to sleep and didn't wake up. He didn't want to live anymore. Nobody expected it, especially not my dad. There's a lot I still meant to say to him, he told me.

And now when we pass Leisure World on the way to the bullfight Dad says, "I always get a pang of emotion here. This exit."

We hear it but don't respond. Nobody wants to talk about anything sad, sentimental, certainly not in front of the photojournalist. We're going to the bullfight.

"Remember the strawberries?" says Dad.

"Sure are a lot of new buildings down here," says Mom. "Your dad would have loved it."

We park at the border, walk through the gate, and catch a taxi to the plaza de toros.

"De donde está usted?" Mom asks the driver.

"South Pasadena."

"Quién es esto?" she says, pointing at a statue of an Indian in a traffic circle.

"Cahuaut—" he starts, "um, I can't remember how to pronounce it."

"Es muy lindo."

"I bet you can guess who this is in the next statue."

"Abraham Lincoln," says Mom with a Spanish accent. She looks at the woven rugs hanging in storefronts and asks the driver if he knows a good wholesaler. "Quiero comprar en bulk."

I knew I had misjudged my parents as sponsors of this excursion when we pulled into the gas station five blocks from home and Dad reached into his hidden money belt—we were going to Mexico, after all—and revealed that he'd only brought fifty dollars for the whole day. Mom had twenty, so I paid for the gas.

At the bullring tickets cost twenty-eight dollars and they don't take Visa. I had hoped to treat Hannah, but instead I have to ask her to loan me a twenty. With all my parents' money spent, we walk down the boulevard looking for a restaurant that takes credit cards. I've never taken them to dinner, or lunch, or breakfast. I don't even bother to offer. I never have any money. But today they forgot their money, so when the bill comes I pay it. It feels sort of new, sort of adult. Maybe it will impress Hannah. Some drunk Americans are shouting and swearing in another booth, and Mom tells them to can it. Dad is embarrassed.

Any hopes I had of appearing a true aficionado are wrecked the instant the toreros parade into the ring. Just as I am explaining to Hannah the difference between a rejoneador and a picador, Mom says: "Don't tell them I said so, but I think those boys ought to wear a better jock supporter. It's all hanging off to the side."

Squinting into Dad's zoom lens, Mom declares that the matadors in their tight little suits and pink socks are quite hunky. The bullfighters wave one arm while the other rests in its embroidered sling.

"A novillero," I tell Hannah, "is an amateur who hopes one day to be confirmed as a matador."

"One of them has a broken arm," says Mom. "I wonder if they'll let him perform. Wait: They all have broken arms."

This is very terrible. She is not my mother. Yes, that's it, she's just some dotty old lady from Anaheim who happened to sit beside me. Relieved of that burden I tap Hannah on the shoulder and explain what a banderillero does.

"Olé!" shouts Mom. "Oh. I guess I'm not supposed to say that yet. Looky there! That man has a prosthetic leg. He must have been gored by a bull."

The Slovak photojournalist gets up and jumps to the front row to take pictures. Safely out of earshot. I look around to see if anyone else can hear my mother.

"Do you think the matadors walk like that all the time," asks Mom, "or just when they wear those suits? They could get a back problem."

Mom's favorite parts are when the bull is winning, and she announces that in her opinion "the guy should get charged more often." Just then the bullfighter loses his cape, sprints to the wall and leaps over to safety, landing in a heap on the concrete.

"Olé!" cries Mom. "Olé!"

Then, noticing that nobody else is saying Olé, she says, "Oops. I guess you're not supposed to cheer for the bull."

I buy a five-dollar cigar, thinking maybe Dad and I will share it, a father-and-son moment, but he makes a face and shakes his head, so I smoke the whole thing myself, feeling a bit sick afterward. I am doing my best to stick it out with Mom and Dad, but I finally snap when they point out how much the bull looks like my dog.

"He has such a sweet face," says Mom. "He looks at that cape just like Tuffy looks at her ball. He thinks it's a game."

"Do you think it gets confused?" says Dad.

And when the blood begins to drip into the sand, Mom says, "He doesn't want to play anymore."

After the third bull is killed, Hannah wants to know what they do with the carcasses. We descend the stairs and there beneath the bleachers find the dead animal that's been dragged from the ring. Children bend down to touch his warm body. Then someone says muevate, muevate, and they drag him by the tail and the neck-chain onto the wet concrete floor of the butcher's room. Blood is everywhere, guts fill a bucket. The skinless heads whisper in a huddle and big black hearts thump in stew.

Hannah starts clicking photos. When a security guard approaches I think he's going to tell us we can't take pictures, but instead he offers me a mounted set of bull horns for fifteen dollars. Special price, he says.

The butchers are *shick-shick*ing their knives on sharpening dowels that dangle from their waists. They whack off the front legs, then slit the belly like a piece of upholstery, expelling a waft of steam. The skin peels off white and fatty on the inside.

And here's the best part: There's a crowd gathering to watch. Not gawking tourists or weirdos in overcoats, but regular people, families. A little girl on her father's shoulders cries, "Mommy, they're cutting off the head!" Sure, the bullfighters had artistry and tragedy and all that, but it's about time these backstage specialists get their spotlight.

These craftsmen do all the dirty work while the primping matadors, just like those vain, shirtless river guides, get all the credit.

Now the butcher has sliced through the neck muscles, and he produces a meat cleaver bigger than a timber axe, and—*whack, whack*—we can hear the neck bone sever, and he kicks the head, which wobbles to where the others are gathered, landing upside down with an eye missing. The stench of entrails washes over us, some squirmy little things like jumbo prawn are set aside on a tin tray, and everyone is grinning, giddy, pushed up against the gate like it's a rock concert. Inside, men in suits look very important hopping away from splashing fluids, hiking up their pant cuffs, bending down to the skulls and counting teeth, jotting notes on a clipboard.

The butchers hack at the corpse, scooping out the organs with bare hands. Their shirts and hats are smeared with blood. They don't care: It's just blood. They never smile, so spellbound by their own creativity. Now they cut notches in the bull's ankles and hoist him spread-legged and pink from the floor. Someone drags out a little two-step staircase—something you'd see in a circus for the sheepdog to climb onto the tightrope—and the butcher with the magnificent cleaver climbs the steps and wields it over his head and brings it down hard on the coccyx. We're all rapt, and *thwack* is the sound echoing from the meat room down the plaza tunnel. Then ándale, ándale, the door swings open and here come two butchers pushing a big vat of something on a rickety cart, heavy enough to bog down in the horse-piss mud, and we all lean over to see what's inside—we have to see what's inside!—and pull back with a grimace because wouldn't you know it's a thirty-gallon

*Deaf to the thundering Olé from the bullring above,
the carnicero plies his noble craft.*

drum of cow shit, bursting from the intestines, just like
those boxes of shit I empty at my job. I have finally found
my brothers in art, brothers in spirit.

The butchers wave Hannah into the room and she keeps shooting, tiptoeing around the blood and never looking out from behind the lens. They love her, a city girl in high-heeled boots snapping their photo. They pose with the skinless head, hoist the sides of beef on their shoulder, flash a thumbs-up to her camera. Mira la corazón, one tells her, clutching the purple blob in his fist. When it's finished Hannah stumbles out into the daylight looking a bit pale.

"I got hit by a flying piece of meat," she says. "I almost barfed."

In the bullring the crowd roars in ecstasy. I've heard it before: the sound of great bullfighting happening while I'm in the men's room or snack shack or out in the tunnel for fresh air. I think I should go watch, but then Hannah tells the butchers I'm writing a book, and the guy whose job it is to lug the beef onto the truck demands to be interviewed. So while the matador is killing with a single graceful thrust, I'm outside the meat truck learning about Oscar Rodriguez. He's from the state of Guanojuato but has lived in Tijuana most of his life. He loves his job. Most of the butchers are brothers, who cut bulls alongside their father, who's been doing this forty-one years. During the week Oscar is a garbage man, and he's worked the Sunday bull-fights for sixteen years. He gets paid fifteen dollars.

"An hour?"

"A day."

"A whole day?"

"As long as it takes for the six bulls."

"That's not too bad."

"The money's not important," says Oscar. "I do it because it's fun."

"Me too."

He stands on a scale hoisting the side of beef on his shoulder, and someone jots down the weight in a little notebook. The four hunks of bull are tallied to weigh 350 kilos, which means, he explains, that the guts, skin, head, and hooves weigh about 150. The meat is not sold, he says, but donated to drug addicts in rehab centers, and also to orphanages.

As we talk the crowd's roaring continues. Judging by the intensity, the fight is over and the judge has ordered at least one ear cut and the matador is making a lap in the sand, kissing hats and flinging them back to the seats. The tunnel doors swing open and a boy pushes a wheelbarrow from the ring and dumps a heap of blood-soaked sand. A little girl is trying to sell a bull's ear in a beer cup. The butchers drip blood and sharpen knives and pose for pictures, then the harnessed horses charge through, dragging the next bull, and it's time to get back to work.

We cross the border with ten dollars to spare and float north past the dark bluffs of Camp Pendleton to the big globe reactors at San Onofre. Mom decides she wants a Jamba Juice so we get off the freeway at El Toro and circle the parking lots of the Spanish-tile strip mall. But there's no Jamba Juice, and besides it's ten o'clock on a Sunday night and places are closed. There are a few burger drive-thrus but Mom and Hannah don't want to eat beef after the day's activities.

"We could go to a sit-down place," says Dad. "There's a Fuddruckers."

"I'm too tired."

"What do you feel like having?"

"I'm not very hungry."

"Me neither."

Finally we pull up behind AM/PM and get juice and chocolate milk and a big cookie wrapped in cellophane. Dad's hungry, though, so after I give him five bucks he lopes across the boulevard and returns with a Jumbo Jack and curly fries, which he eats out of the bag in the backseat as I pull into the diamond lane. By the time we reach Irvine Mom and Dad are asleep with their heads against the headrests, mouths slightly open, the white bag of wrappers and napkins crumpled on Dad's lap, and as I drive them home the freeway is fluid and smooth, lots of cars but we're moving good, no delays, office lights twinkling in the glass blocks of the business parks, a light mist settling everywhere and the jets overhead cleared for landing at John Wayne International. I guess this is what we call freedom. And with nobody looking I'll admit it, yes, I loved Orange County, with its fields of strawberries and Hot Dog on a Stick, its smooth culs-de-sac and terra-cotta roofs, and I loved Leisure World for its shuffleboard afternoons at Clubhouse Number Four and its green, green fairways where my brother and I learned to drive a golf cart. Those were the days and the sun always shone. Everyone's seat belt is fastened, and here in the fast lane I am safe and peaceful and, in a way I did not expect, a part of my own family.

CHAPTER THIRTEEN

STALKING IS A STRONG WORD, AND IF THAT'S
what historians choose to call my moving to the same
block as Hannah Kjoprczak, they should reconsider. My
friend Henry left town for a month and let me stay in his
room. By then I needed to vacate Mom and Dad's place.
The publisher's attorney had tracked me to their address,
and I'd received a curt letter accusing breach of contract
and demanding I return the advance. But the money was
long since spent, and more to the point, the book was almost complete, in a version far superior to what they'd
paid for. They were getting literature at pulp prices, and I
refused to give anything back.

Most important, I had Hannah. The love between her
and Travis was blossoming quickly on paper, and I rea-
soned that a real-life tryst would soon follow. In the end,
love would prevail. Hannah would deliver a romantic cli-
max for *Toro* more triumphant than anything Spain could
offer. But any carnal attraction we felt—and hers for me
was certainly considerable—was secondary to the Work:
My intention for the Slovak was nothing short of redeeming
a masterpiece and validating the genius of Travis LaFrance.
In short, she would save me.

My new home was on a shady green hill in view of the downtown high-rises, overlooking the flat train yards and freeways along the concrete river. The roads were steep and curvy and birds sang in the trees all night long, imitating the wail of police sirens and car alarms. The first thing I did each morning was look out the window for Hannah's lovely Volkswagen bug parked on the street. If it wasn't there she had spent the night with her boyfriend, and I'd get to work on *Toro*. If it was there, I'd scout for his motorcycle. The big chopper with a huge chain lock meant he'd spent the night, and I'd shut my bedroom door and plunge into the book.

But this morning the Beetle was there alone. My excitement was delicious, and knowing that she kept a carton of milk in her fridge, I could not survive without a splash for my tea. I had a full quart of my own in the kitchen, but I wisely decided it smelled bad and poured it down the sink, and I dialed her number and she said come over and bring your cup. I ducked beneath the honeysuckle and pushed the creaky gate and crept quivering along the house brushing spiderwebs from my face. I tiptoed up the staircase to prove I wasn't too eager. Down the hillside the morning rush on the Golden State Freeway roared like the surf. The sun burned brightly through the haze.

Hannah was just out of the shower, and her camisole was wet at the collarbone where her hair fell. As I pushed through the door she was hopping on one foot on the linoleum, tugging at her jeans. Coffee steamed on the stove.

"Either I got fat or I washed them too hot."

She squatted low and stretched and hiked up the denim and buttoned the button. My plastic mug trembled.

"They put in a goddamn hand-scan at work," she said. "As if we were going to lie about our hours."

"Milk?" I said.

"Next thing you know they'll give us a cavity search on the way out. I've worked there a year and never even a raise."

I poured the milk in my cup.

"I'd hoped that by the time I was thirty-three I wouldn't have to punch a time card."

She wiggled in her jeans, poured her coffee, and stepped into a pair of flip-flops.

"I can sort of breathe now," she said. "Hey, what was the date for Mexicali?"

"Two weeks."

"Count me in."

And once she'd driven off to work I rushed to my room to write. I invented for Hannah a dramatic life story: Persecuted for her politics in her homeland, she has escaped as a mail-order bride, purchased by a cruel American who attempts to enslave her. Sacrificing the citizenship he's promised, Hannah leaves him and finds menial work in a Los Angeles photo lab, determined to pursue her art. But the owner of the lab is a lecher who flicks his tongue and promises her a green card if she'll spend five years in his darkroom, if you know what I mean. When our story begins, Hannah is daydreaming of a real American man like she's read about in books who'll deliver her from captivity and carry her to a workers' paradise.

Enter Travis LaFrance.

I try to think up an ending. I pace and sit and stand and stare all day, and at dusk I hear the unmistakable rattle of her Volkswagen climbing the hill. I carry a bag of trash to the curb, but the rattle belongs to someone else's Beetle. Well, no reason to leave this garbage out where the varmints might get it. I take it back in and lie on the couch. A half-hour passes before the tiny motor putts up the hill and I remember I need to check the pressure of my tires. I go to the street and study my truck until she opens her door, plastic bottles and paper cups bouncing on the asphalt. She gathers up her fabulous suede handbag and boxes of photos, and with car keys jangling calls hello. I look up like I'm surprised.

"Is that you, Hannah? I didn't notice you pull in."

"You'll never guess what I did today."

"I was just out here working on my truck."

"I asked for a raise. I told him I wanted fifteen an hour but I'd settle for twelve-fifty."

"I do all the work on this truck myself."

"It was easier than I thought it'd be. He said fine and he'd tell me the exact amount tomorrow."

"What are you doing tonight?"

"Going over to Danny's, I guess."

I twist a cap off the tire stem and take a reading. The sky is red. Hannah jingles her car keys again. She can't be expected to grasp the importance of each minute spent with Travis LaFrance. The pressure gauge says twenty-eight.

"Well, I'll talk to you later," she says.

"This one's going to need a little air."

"What?"

"Never mind," I say. "I wasn't talking to you."

She shifts from foot to foot, becoming a silhouette as the day ends.

"Don't forget it's trash night," she says.

"What?"

"The trash man comes tomorrow."

"I don't have any trash. But thanks anyway."

I have an idea for an ending that will quench Hannah's thirst for a getaway with Travis. I learn that the farm towns of central California hold Portuguese bullfights. I'm not sure what that means, but it's only a day's drive and puts her safely out of the gaze of her man.

But Hannah says she won't go. She thinks she shouldn't ask for time off work just after getting a raise, and besides, she and Danny have plans. I don't ask for what. Hannah isn't turning out as free-spirited as the Slovak photojournalist I invented. My heroine doesn't have to work when she is needed ringside, and she certainly doesn't have a boyfriend she won't drop for a date with Travis. If she doesn't shape up I might have to break up with her.

Without Hannah I don't really want to go to the bullfight. But I can't bear to sit still with the book unfinished and she and Danny together across the street. She has let me down. Fine. Sometimes a man must go it alone. On Friday morning I fill my tires with the appropriate amount of air and pull onto the Golden State Freeway heading north.

There are corridas scheduled for both Friday and Sunday. I drive five rainy hours through the farmlands and cattle ranches to a town called Crow's Nest, ask about the bullfights at the gas station across the street from the rusty mill, receive a few blank looks until one old-timer directs me back across the interstate and into the hills. I find a one-lane dirt track skirting a wastewater plant across a brown pasture where a bowed strip of plywood reads TOROS.

I follow it up through the foothills to where a closed gate says Campo Grande Pico Dos Padres. A man is parked there in a custom van.

"Is this the bullfight?"

"No English," he says, waving his hands. "No speak English."

"Bull. Fight. Here?"

"Cancelado. No English."

I drive ten feet then remember I know Spanish and throw it in reverse.

"Aquí está la corrida?" I ask him.

"No espanish. Cancelado."

"No hablas español?"

"No español. Portugueso."

"Por qué está cancelada la corrida?"

The man holds up his hands and wiggles all fingers to indicate rain. I say gracias and drive away.

Then it hits me that actual Portuguese people run the Portuguese bullfight. I have assumed it's all Mexicans and that Portuguese is some sort of code, the way people say inner-city when they mean black. But now I realize I was wrong, and with a thrill decide this trip will satisfy the publisher's dim insistence on a taste of Europe.

In three days I return for the rescheduled festival. Exiting the interstate I drive right off the map and into a different country. I take the dirt lane past barbed wire and dusty oak groves through a long field until a compound of buildings appears. I park alongside the other trucks on dried cow pies outside a corrugated tin barn. Up on the hillside cows chew the dead grass and lean against a stick fence enclosing a chapel the size of a Fotomat dedicated to Nossa

Senhora do Pilar. The sky is smudged with brown streaks of clouds.

The festival is under way. Portuguese pop music bounces out of a rented speaker set while a hawk circles above and nests atop a power line that runs in a ribbon over the beige California hills. Old cowboys in jeans lean against pickup trucks and talk Portuguese. In the hazy twilight the teenage princesses dance in pairs on a concrete tablet beneath strings of plastic flags. They wear black turtlenecks and rhinestone tiaras and prom-night hairstyles, and they smack bubble-gum as they tote little sisters around the cement dance floor. A cowboy waltzes his wife.

I wouldn't have been surprised to go my whole life without hearing Portuguese spoken, but here I am minutes off the freeway transported to Europe. Everyone over thirty is speaking Portuguese. The publisher is going to love this. I sit at the food counter beside a man with a trumpet case and a windbreaker that says Livingston Portuguese Orchestra. Ladies in latex gloves sell food that comes in two choices, and I ask the man what prego is.

"A bread with a meat inside."

"And linguica?"

"It's a tube, a big one, and long."

I order the bread with meat and wish Hannah were here to take pictures. Maybe I'd even ask her to dance. I imagine Travis and Hannah floating across the concrete to the accordion music. They are bold, unafraid to love, even in this foreign outpost.

"Do you like?" says the man with the trumpet. "These are the foods of my country."

"Very good. I like the prego."

"Me: born in San George. Nineteen years in Africa. Twenty-two years here."

"How long have there been bullfights?"

"Beer ticket! Beer ticket!" he shouts, waving a raffle stub. "Like beer you?"

I say I do and he redeems the ticket and sets an icy can before me.

"Now: Festival de Espiritu Santo. English says Festival of Spirit Saint. Very old festival in my country. Very many bullfighting."

"How come?"

"In Portugal is Isabel and Ferdinand. This is many years. He is mean king, but she is good woman. She takes the bread to give to the poor who very hungry. The bread she hides in her dress for the king cannot see it. He will be very angry. He can put her to the death if she do wrong. He see the wife, she go outside the door, and he stop to demand what she has, to return the bread to the castle. But she is a very good woman and she say no bread. The king pull on her clothes, but there no bread, because it turn all to roses red. And this is our miracle of santos, for why we have the festival."

I finish the prego and push the paper plate across the counter. I'll be irked if something once-in-a-lifetime happens and Hannah's not here to photograph it.

"Look: We have a queen of our festival," says the Portuguese, pointing at the teen girls with their braided hair. "And also two princesas."

"How do they get elected?"

"When their father is president of the festival."

"Are you a bullfighter?" I ask.

"No. I am a ranch."

The man picks up his trumpet case and says it is time to go to the ring. I follow. The first thing different about a bullfight in America is that the bull wears velcro. The flags stick between his shoulders without drawing blood. The toreros clench their teeth as they step out from behind the barrera for another set of passes. Because the bulls don't get stabbed, they don't get slow. It's fast and sloppy and dangerous, like the bull could actually win. Old men in derby hats curse in Portuguese as the velcro flags fall in the dirt and the bullfighters scurry to safety. With the matador faking his stabs it's hard to tell when the fight is over. Before he can make his lap they have to chase the bull out of the ring. I ask the man next to me if he comes here a lot, and he waves his hand with a snort.

"Twenty bucks for see this? Ha!"

And now here come the forcadores, a crew of beefy lads dressed as shepherds, and the crowd gets quiet. I'm told they play on the high school football team and their mission is to tackle a bull. The bull charges, and the first one leaps onto the horns like a bicyclist mounting a semi-truck, and in turn the others dogpile until the bull is stopped. The people holler. I think that since everyone here lives in America they prefer a good old-fashioned tackling to some dude in a fancy suit flicking a sword. When it's over a cowboy on a tractor rakes circles in the ring. I leave before the last bullfight and drive fast down the highway toward Los Angeles. At three in the morning Hannah's car is not parked out front.

Neither did Hannah come with me to my bullfighting lesson. I learned about the only English-speaking toreo school in the world, and called up. The owner invited me down to

San Diego for a free class. If this didn't win Hannah over, nothing would. I suggested she photograph me, but as usual she had to work. So I went alone, well before rush hour, and was flushed down the empty freeways to Chula Vista. There was nobody to talk to, or impress, or make up chapters about. I was stuck being me. I couldn't be Travis without her.

What would this bullfighter think of me? Unlike the ones I'd met in Mexico, he was an American who spoke English. He might see through my slumming disguise, and recognize that the holes in my shoes and the primer spots on my truck were a feeble camouflage for a university degree and a life of unspent gringo privilege. I was underdressed. He'd probably be wearing black trousers and a traje corto, look once at my hand-me-down wardrobe—this so-called writer, not respectful enough to shave or brush my hair— then sniff and say something dismissive in Spanish. Well, even if he didn't like me, I'd be getting the authentic experience. Just as a real gymnast learns his craft vaulting barbed wire in Romania and a real soccer player grows up kicking melons in the Brazilian rain forests, now I was headed to the Mexican border to learn the art of the bullring from a master. I needed to look like a writer. I tucked in my shirt.

My journey landed me in the suburbs. I followed smooth new boulevards into the foothills, winding between tracts of condominiums behind stucco walls. It looked like Leisure World. I slowed at the empty gatehouse, rolled over a speed bump, and parked at the curb. The asphalt was smooth and the sidewalks unstained. Green grass had been rolled out like a carpet, and saplings were tied to straight sticks. It was as if I'd opened a children's book and all these town houses had popped up off the page. The bullfighter lived on a cul-de-sac.

Inside, the teacher and the student were drinking cups of water at the dinette. The teacher wore sweatpants and was explaining the pictures in a big glossy book. Plastic race cars were parked on the carpet, and when a boy padded down the stairs the bullfighter asked him to walk the dog. The boy put on his shoes and set out through the back patio toward the golf course.

"Part of what we do is study the culture of the corrida," said the teacher, motioning at the stack of Spanish books. The student was in his final year of law school. He wore khakis and loafers. He told me he'd already killed his first bull, down in Mexico, and it had been a wild and difficult animal. Now he was training for another.

We drove in two cars to the elementary school. A street sign said, "Congrats, Eastlake Greens! Best New Community Four Years Running!" The teacher realized he'd forgotten his sword at home, so he told me to wait in the parking lot while he fetched it. I got out of the truck and stood in the fire lane where it said No Parking. Kids were playing soccer on the grass. This was the kind of place I could get arrested for loitering. "You see, officer," I rehearsed, "I'm waiting here for my bullfighting lesson."

Master and student returned and we began. The cinder-block wall of a curved turnaround was our barrera. The student unfolded his pink and yellow capote. The creases were crisp and straight. He'd forgotten his sneakers, and the teacher scolded him as he practiced his passes in loafers.

"You want success! You don't want to be tossed! You have to think like a torero!"

The student backpedaled over the asphalt with his cape hanging like a starched curtain. A station wagon pulled into our turnaround to collect some children. We got out of the way and let it pass. The student asked if anyone else was coming. The teacher said that Juan Carlos had to work tonight and the others didn't call back. The teacher demonstrated a proper veronica.

"Who's the one who does it this way?"

"Um . . ."

"Remember from the video."

The student did not remember.

"It was José Tomás."

"Right. José Tomás."

Then I got the cape. It was heavier than I expected. I swayed behind it, trotting backward. As the teacher charged me with horns I made grunt noises and wondered if they sounded right. I felt the evening dew on my brow. The cape rippled at my feet and pulled heavily on my shoulders. It felt almost real, and the only thing missing was Hannah. If she were here popping flashbulbs she'd see through her lens more than a guy waving a cloth in a cul-de-sac. She'd see Travis. The streetlight's flicker would be the glow of an oil lantern, the crickets on the soccer field would be singing from the campo bravo, and if we squinted just right at the terra-cotta tract houses, just like that we'd be together in Spain.

I need an ending. I need to get Hannah anywhere that has anything to do with bulls. I take her to Griffith Park on Saturday morning to watch the men practice toreo. The men take off their shirts and work in pairs. Hannah takes pictures. Before long they break out the Tecate and a bottle of sherry from the south of Spain.

"It's dry," says the pourer.

"Very dry," concurs Travis.

We sit on the grass and drink. Practice is over. The toreros ask if we are aficionados. They want to know why she's taking pictures. I tell them that certainly I am an aficionado: I'm Travis LaFrance, author of the work in progress *Toro*; perhaps they've read my other work. No one has, but before long I've collected a small docket of business cards, phone numbers, suggested books, and e-mail addresses.

They all have bullfighting stories to tell. And even though I'm the writer of adventure books, they're telling their stories to Hannah. When she laughs and tosses her hair you see freckles on her forehead and feel lucky to have seen them, like you've been granted a privilege that others are denied. The men invite her to join them at the park every Saturday, invite her to Tijuana, invite her to their taurine club dinner. Like me they've been to a bullfight alone and know it's so much better with a lady along to cover her eyes at the sight of the blood. That's the best part. They don't mind when she doesn't know the names of the matadors or when she mispronounces picador. They want to talk to her.

"When I see the matador in his suit of lights," says Paco the Ecuadorian, who is fifty years old and wears a golf shirt, "he is a prince. He is like a prince to me."

But they can't have her. She's mine. I discovered her. She's going to Mexicali with me tomorrow morning. My date. My female lead. I wonder if she's ready to leave her man for me. She never talks about him, and I never ask. Maybe she knows not to discuss the inevitable.

After I drop her at home, I sit at my desk and think

about our trip tomorrow. Just she and I at a bullfight. And suddenly *Toro*'s ending descends on me from heaven. Travis and Hannah: together in Mexicali. I put them in a cheap motel room. Tawdry. I plant a finger on the road map and determine their union will occur in the dusty border town of Calexico, measuring one part international flair with two parts run-down crumminess. The bullfight will end at eleven o'clock, so it will be midnight before they cross the border. Hannah will fall asleep, slumping in the bench seat of Travis's full-sized pickup truck. He'll draw her near with a callused finger and she'll doze for a moment on his lap, the desert air rushing through the cab. They'll drive for a while like this, so maybe I'll have to move them to a hotel in El Centro, the next town past Calexico. Anyway, after a bit of sleep, she, along with years of latent animal desire, will awaken in Travis's lap, and without a word he'll flip the blinker and veer into Los Amantes Motor Lodge, a desperate cracked-plaster piece of Americana with a muscle car propped on cinder blocks in the lot. Pulling back the lemon-scented bedsheets while a delicate smoke-stream lifts from a lone cigarette in the ashtray, Travis will penetrate the elegant femininity of the Old World while the Slovak beauty yields to the inevitable strength of a global superpower.

It's very good. The phone rings, but I don't answer. I keep writing. The entire day has passed. I haven't eaten. But it's a very good chapter: *Toro* has an ending. The publisher gets his book. Travis gets the girl.

I package the manuscript and barrel my bike down the hill to Echo Park and deliver it to the post office.

"Priority," I say to the postmaster, and with a clang of a register and the thunk of a rubber stamp, *Toro* departs the shelter of its creator and begins its journey to the world canon.

Back on my bike I hop the curbs on Sunset Boulevard to a taco shack where I lean on the counter and celebrate with carnitas and an Orange Bang. The sun is shining, and this afternoon Los Angeles is a fine city leaping up to congratulate me. I pedal my bike up to the old Victorians in Angeleno Heights, where some kids in undershirts are working in a driveway under the hood of a car. I wave hello. I ride along the Korean storefronts on Sunset, then against traffic to the deserted alleys of Chinatown, then back up to the hill past Dodger Stadium. Gunshots from the police academy salute me in the ravine. I coast into the Valley, down graffitied streets and chain-link dead ends to the path along the concrete river, where the water is green with algae and smells like mulch as it winds through willows and boulders and rusted skeletons of shopping carts.

This is your town, Travis. You've made it.

CHAPTER FOURTEEN

———

HANNAH AND I APPROACH THE BORDER. A thermometer in El Centro says 110. I'm glad I have my little Japanese pickup with air conditioner rather than Travis's '65 Chevy with the windows open. We've driven across the desert early so that Hannah can do some shopping before the corrida. She'd like to get some rawhide for the cover of her portfolio, and maybe some silver earrings. We cross into Mexico in downtown Mexicali. Hannah skims through a travel guide she's brought. "Says here that Mexicali is a desolate industrial border town with nothing to do."

We drive the streets looking for a plaza where mariachis sing and margaritas are blended and vendors hock serapes folded over their arms. We're in Mexico, after all. But there are no mariachis. The sidewalks are blackened from exhaust, and the beer ads painted on buildings peel in the sun. In the tienda windows we see ladies' shoes and clock radios and soccer jerseys. It's Sunday and the shops are shuttered with metal grates. Shoeshine men have wheeled their carts into the shade and sit there lifelessly. The sunlight hurts. Rolling down the window is like inserting your head into an oven. I park the car in the shadow of a two-story building with a laundromat on the ground floor. We have four hours before the bullfight starts.

So far Hannah has shown no sign of knowing what lies in store at the end of the book. I watch her click down the sidewalk in search of a popsicle. Tonight at the motor lodge she will not only secure her place in the canon but also end my voyeurism. No more sitting around dreaming about Travis LaFrance and his harem; beginning tonight I am him.

To begin the transformation I change clothes. There in the front seat I wiggle out of shorts and sandals and into jeans and boots. I even put on a cowboy hat. When Hannah returns I'm enthroned on the shoeshine cart and I try to show off by talking Spanish to the wrinkled man who's buffing my boots.

"Siempre hace calor en mayo?"

"Sí, hace calor en mayo."

"Y junio?"

"Hace calor en augusto tambien."

"Julio tiene más calor de todo?"

"Sí."

"Y como está septiembre?"

"Septiembre es más caliente que todo."

We find a hotel with a bar and order two beers. We're the only ones there. The air-conditioning makes it feel like an airport. It would be a bit more exotic if, out the window, we could see something other than the American border crossing. I drink the beer as slowly as I can because I can't afford another.

At the bullring we buy the middle-priced tickets. This is my idea, because in Mexico City and Tijuana you can sneak to the front row and nobody bothers you. The heat is astounding. Everyone is flapping a paper fan with a picture of the guy running for mayor, but it doesn't make it any cooler, it just gives you something to think about. A crowd has gathered in the shade of a towering inflatable beer can. We join a circle watching flamenco dancers. Mascara drips from their cheeks and splats on the plywood. Hannah squats in front of me with her camera. I watch beads of sweat form on the small of her back and roll down her spine and disappear into her jeans. All the men standing beside me are watching the same thing, so I force my eyes elsewhere.

Our seats are so high that Hannah can't take pictures. There's no way to sneak to the front. The concrete benches burn the backs of my legs. We cook in the concrete oven, slump over the railing like melted food.

"If you want," I say, "we'll go down to the ticket office and get the expensive seats."

I'm bluffing. I don't have enough money to trade up. But I'm pretty sure she's not going to want to do anything that requires moving. She rubs her eyes and peels away the strands of hair stuck to her neck, then says something that sounds like, "Bluh."

Then the first bull charges the arena and I realize that between me and Los Amantes Motor Lodge are six bulls to be dispatched. After seeing sixty bulls badly killed in my short career as an aficionado I hardly have the stomach to watch six more botches. So I've crafted my final chapter with bullfighting that is smooth and graceful. I hope the kills are decent.

The toreros heed my wishes. The matador spins on his toes and dances on his knees. Hannah sets down her camera and watches. Olé after Olé thunders from the crowd just as it should for the finale of a bullfighting book, and even though the first thing I think of is television salsa commercials, the

We are the hollow men
We are the stuffed men
—T. S. Eliot

hair on my neck still rises. The matador points his sword and
sinks it, and the bull, as if knowing this is the climactic chapter, stumbles three steps and falls. White napkins blossom
in the stands and the crowd hollers at the judge and he
hangs two handkerchiefs and the knife man cuts two ears.
The matador struts around the ring brandishing the back of
his hand like an opera singer, basking in his triumph, cele-
brating his debut into the works of Travis LaFrance.

All evening the matadors sparkle beneath the grand-
stand lights. The bulls fall on my command, the people
shout for ears, the ladies in the front row toss roses. It's
just like I've written it. The scene is set for Los Amantes as
Hannah and I sweat in the front seat of the truck waiting to

cross the border. It's almost midnight and ninety-five degrees. Idling there I cut off the air conditioner so the truck
won't overheat. In Calexico it's too early to stop at a motel
so we get doughnuts instead.

"Dos old-fashioned y uno glazed," says Travis LaFrance.

We drive across the desert with the warm wind blasting
through the windows. Hannah should be getting tired any
minute now, going limp and asking to lean against my
shoulder. Pretty soon she'll ask if I'm too sleepy to drive,
and suggest that she call in sick in the morning.

"Tired?" I say.

"Not really."

She sits upright and lights a cigarette. We're silent.
Something is troubling her. She's thinking about what to
say to me. She'll probably begin with something like: Travis,
these last couple weeks have been very special.

"I meant to ask you," she finally says. I turn the radio off.

"Yes, Hannah?"

"What about the morality of it?"

She's conflicted about leaving her man for me. That's
understandable. She just needs to talk it over.

"Tell me what you mean," I say.

"I mean: killing all those bulls. Just for a show. Isn't
there something wrong with that?"

Oh, metaphor! She's comparing our love to a bullfight.
Yes, love is brutal. But when one thing dies, another is created.

"But it's art," I say. "The bull gives its life to make
something beautiful."

"That's great for the bullfighters. But we're not bullfighters. We just pay our money and sit in the stands and
watch. Where's the art in that?"

I keep driving. Not even Travis LaFrance can think of a way that watching a bullfight is art.

"I feel so guilty watching those bulls get killed," says Hannah. "Don't you?"

"Sometimes. But as soon as I cross the border it goes away."

She says nothing.

"It's Mexico," I reason. "You can do whatever you want in Mexico, and as soon as you get home it's all erased."

We crest a hill and look west to the glow of San Diego. I'd better change the subject if I'm going to get the final chapter falling into place.

"How are things with you and Danny?" I say.

"They're good. We're looking for a place to move in together."

She says it matter-of-factly, as if she'd already made the decision, end of discussion, without even consulting me.

"Moving in? Isn't that a bit drastic?"

"If it were up to me I'd take him to Vegas and marry him. But he wants to wait till we pay off some debts. It makes more sense that way."

"That's crazy. You're too young."

"I'm thirty-three."

"What about adventure?"

"I had those when I was young."

Finally she gets tired and leans against the window and closes her eyes. She's asleep as we zip along the San Diego freeway, the way she's supposed to be in my book, but by now it's too late. She's ruined it. She can still be immortalized in *Toro*, still have her eternal fling with Travis at Los Amantes, but in this life she'll settle for a long, late drive and three hours' sleep before the alarm clock buzzes. Instead of a dissident Slovak photojournalist she'll be another American working forty hours a week. Instead of a white-hot fling with a fledgling author she'll marry someone she loves.

And I'll have to settle for watching from the stands instead of performing in the ring. I'll settle for another two hours floating over freeways and a lapful of tacos from an all-night drive-thru, and I'll settle for walking Hannah to her honeysuckle gate at four in the morning while the neighborhood birds sing the songs of car alarms. And when I awake alone and it's time to write, I'll settle for fiction, for a story that never happened, for inventing the life of Travis LaFrance because the one I live won't last forever and isn't good enough for books.

The freeway funnels toward Los Angeles. Hannah sleeps with her head lolling forward. Now is the time when Travis would draw her close and kiss her cheek. She's asleep. She has no idea. I reach behind the seat for a pillow and prop it behind her head. Hannah leans against it and sleeps. This is the best I can do.

ACKNOWLEDGMENTS

The Western Canon owes a debt to Mathew Gross and Melony Gilles, who were the first to recognize *Toro* as a book unlike any written before it. Literature would not have arrived where it is today without the guidance of Eric Puchner, Jeffrey Libby, Angie Stover, Erik Bluhm, Franklin Seal, Gabe Weiss, and Rae Meadows. The Republic of Mexico should honor its citizens Miguel Calderon, Jacobo Medina, and the Vargas Valadez family for their hospitality extended to a legendary expatriate. And literary historians fortunate enough to record the creation of this work will applaud New York alchemists Richard Abate, Brando Skyhorse, and Geoffrey Kloske, who turned author's ore into reader's gold.

ABOUT THE AUTHOR

Mark Sundeen was born in 1970 in Harbor City, California. He is the author of *Car Camping*, and co-founder of *Great God Pan* magazine. He lives in Utah.